About the Author

The author has always loved reading and writing. Through books as a child, he saw a world beyond his small town that was closer in imagination than reality. It wasn't until at the age of nine when he visited in a summer one of his older sisters who had left home and lived in a few states over to the east, that his eyes opened wide to the possibility that he could step beyond the boundaries of known geography into what at first and for many years was unknown forbidden territory.

The Looking Glass of the Past

Soni Butterfly

The Looking Glass of the Past

Olympia Publishers
London

www.olympiapublishers.com
OLYMPIA PAPERBACK EDITION

Copyright © Soni Butterfly 2024

The right of Soni Butterfly to be identified as author of
this work has been asserted in accordance with sections 77 and 78 of
the Copyright, Designs and Patents Act 1988.

All Rights Reserved

No reproduction, copy or transmission of this publication
may be made without written permission.
No paragraph of this publication may be reproduced,
copied or transmitted save with the written permission of the publisher,
or in accordance with the provisions
of the Copyright Act 1956 (as amended).

Any person who commits any unauthorised act in relation to
this publication may be liable to criminal
prosecution and civil claims for damage.

A CIP catalogue record for this title is
available from the British Library.

ISBN: 978-1-80439-765-7

This is a work of fiction.
Names, characters, places and incidents originate from the writer's
imagination. Any resemblance to actual persons, living or dead, is
purely coincidental.

First Published in 2024

Olympia Publishers
Tallis House
2 Tallis Street
London
EC4Y 0AB

Printed in Great Britain

Dedication

I dedicate this book to my mom, Henretta, and my daddy, Prell as they rest in peace.

Acknowledgements

My family-wife, Michelle, two daughters, Briana, and Jasonica, and my brothers, sisters, uncles, aunts, cousins, and grandparents are owed a debt of gratitude for keeping me honest about who I am and my potential to become surprisingly a better human being each day along life's journey.

Chapter One

It was a time to remember and a time to forget. In short-term, it was all Uncle Charlie could think about, but in the long-term, it was the one thing he hoped would be difficult to withdraw from his memory bank. The scene was a mess. The ground underneath him, spongy, squishy, soaked in a semi bright, but not completely red coloured slime. There was no time to check to see if the bullet had gone straight through or if it was lodged close to a vital organ. The smell of burnt metal was in the air. Crack and whizzing within range of his left ear at early light as he held the assault rifle, the M-16 compressed to his rapidly beating heart and unclogged arteries, ammunition was flying and dropping in close proximity, too close for comfort. Return fire was timely and cautious.

Seared in his consciousness, faces and lives that mattered more than his own, more than the burst of bombs witnessed around him, darted, across his brain waves every millisecond. His girls and boys were his life and still would be, he believed, if he survived the hell on earth. In a prayer, he promised to tell them that he loved them more. In his imagination, as if in a mind melding, Aunt Ruthie could hear that prayer and she joined along with him in chorus.

What he didn't know, back home, she was living her own hell on earth. Her heart was at a breaking point. Darkness was about to storm the gates. Battle lines had been drawn and her mind experienced a cracking and whizzing of explosive grief.

In a deep, raspy voice, *"are you my God-sent husband?"* Thirty-something and eccentric, my great Aunt Ruthie, with bated breath waited for an answer from the supposed stranger who knocked softly from the other side of the door, who was now quietly backing away and soon about faced, turned towards the porch's screen door. The voice caught the visitor off guard. He was expecting my great grandmother's cheery voice to spill through the chipped paint and cracked edges of a front door that had seen better days. It stayed shut. The unexpected voice behind it, silent. The uneasy visitor nervously moved towards the porch's exit. The porch's screen door opened momentarily. Soon, he was gone.

As the spring of the screen door retracted, allowing the door to close slowly with a soft spooky, creaking sound, Aunt Ruthie slumped forward, her head resting with a thump against the old heavy door that locked from the inside, five steps from the screen door. Lonely, heartbroken, she had not been the same since Uncle Charlie left for Vietnam two years prior. The war was over. Most of his army buddies had returned to their spouses and partners, but Uncle Charlie was missing in action or something like that. Not many people in the community knew what was meant by the coined phrase, missing in action (MIA). Our family knew that it meant that the government didn't know where Uncle Charlie was and if he was alive or dead.

The government wrote a letter about regretting him being lost, but it didn't say much else. It left much to the imagination. Shrouded in technical military jargon, Aunt Ruthie needed an interpreter to explain every other line. *"MIA, what's MIA?"* Her face turned sideways with eyes narrowing in serious attention to every detail spoken by the Vietnam Veteran neighbour, who offered to help explain what the army had written to Aunt Ruthie and her four young children. She had served as an Army nurse in Vietnam, but wasn't drafted, she volunteered. Fifteen months and ten days later she was back home, shell-shocked and suffering effects of Agent Orange. Aunt Ruthie's only friend, she comforted Aunt Ruthie, while putting her own physical and mental health needs second. My great grandmother asked the kind nurse to spend the night when the letter came because Aunt Ruthie seemed more agitated than usual, the madness seemed to gain the upper hand.

That night, Aunt Ruthie lay face down on the floor of the small living room, in between the second-hand coffee table and lumpy, three-legged sofa, crying repeatedly, *"where is my God-sent husband?"* A waterfall showered both cheeks, as her voice grew raspier with each moment of mourning. Her hair usually a neatly, beautiful, stunning tightly curled smooth texture, was uncombed, matted with carpet fibers and her skin glistened with Vaseline. Soiling herself, the pretty flower printed dress was ruined, it reeked of watery feces, sweat and urine. Her dress was removed, her body was washed, but what to do to fix her heart and mind, no one knew. A mental health issue was that thing we didn't discuss in our family. It was taboo. A person was crazy because something spiritual was going on within them and they had to work it out or get help from the church people, preferably someone gifted and experienced with spiritual matters.

Spiritual or not, there is not an easy fix for the mourner's broken heart and mind. Aunt Ruthie knew this too well and lived a tortured life from the moment it was revealed that Uncle Charlie's whereabouts were unknown. To her, it was unfathomable to misplace a whole person. Often heard mumbling under-breath, *"the army lost him, I want him found, now, now. Gitt'm home. I need him, Lord."*

This wasn't her first rodeo with grappling with lost. She had lost things that were important to her before. There were people too, kinfolk and those that she felt a kindred spirit to, who she wished were back in her life, but this was her first MIA lost. How strange it felt. Only others who have experienced that kind of lost could understand her emotional pain and struggle to remain whole in mind and heart.

No one could have prepared Aunt Ruthie for the occurrence of numbness in each limb of her frail body and the intermittent moments of catatonic stillness that overcame her after waking each morning from a deep eventful coma-like sleep. She could never explain the out of body experience and journey taken each night. The physical part of her left behind while the part of her that was immaterial freely roamed wherever and whenever. Temporarily free of the prison that held her captive, it seemed that she was strangely happy and at peace in subconsciousness.

Awaking to reality and outside of unconsciousness, disappointment took hold as she experienced the awareness that she was back in the house that held so many memories of past joy and satisfaction. Her old life was now a figment of her imagination. The first thoughts each morning where of *"the God-sent husband. Where is he, that sexy man who gets me, loves me unconditionally."*

"For better or for worse and till death do us part," were powerfully romantic words with spiritual overtone to them. *"What God brings together, let no man put asunder,"* was comforting when she heard Uncle Charlie say them aloud on that magical day. It was the beginning of a beautifully marital relationship and the rest of their fairy tale life. In hindsight, no

part of her life felt as real as that moment. Before meeting Uncle Charlie, life consisted of just one daydream after another. Most were deep imaginings of what it would be like to be important to someone or matter to more than one person in her small town, a place that seemed insignificant to the rest of the world, but one that would always be home.

Small town lifers were known for their short life-lines that crisscrossed in the right hand palm. Dreamers, their lives cut short, usually by their own hand, distress, or by another person's. A lifer, Aunt Ruthie's oldest sister Molly was murdered. Before Uncle Charlie, the demise of Molly was the first devastating lost Aunt Ruthie had experienced, and the earliest signs of heart fragility began to show.

Headaches, high blood pressure, and chest pain were the physical culprits that made life physically unbearable often. However, the declining mental health didn't make living any easier either. Family matriarch, my great grandmother held monthly meetings with my great uncles and aunts about Aunt Ruthie's state of emotion and physical health because great grandmother didn't think Aunt Ruthie would live very long, but she was wrong. Aunt Ruthie outlived her seemingly heathier brother, my grandfather and his wife/my grandma Etta.

In fact, Aunt Ruthie helped take care of my dad, JT, when Grandma Etta became sick and when she later died because Grandpop had to work a lot of long hours to provide gently used clothing, struggle meals, and a safe place to reside for dad, and his older brothers and sisters. Caring for her four children and my dad gave Aunt Ruthie a purpose on the days she seemed most well. When most lucid, she was the best aunt my dad could ever have. Friendly, protective, and loving, dad enjoyed their time together, there was an understanding between them.

He didn't understand why he wasn't able to see her all the time. No one really explained it either. *"Not today. Maybe tomorrow. We'll see,"* were the words used most often in reply to his request to see her.

After a while, he was only able to see her every other month. Growing curious and older, he asked why and wouldn't stop asking until he felt the answer was good enough. His oldest sister finally told him that Aunt Ruthie was sick and has been back and forth to the hospital in the big city about 80 miles away. *"What's wrong with her,"* dad asked. *"Something is wrong with her brain and emotions,"* his oldest sister replied.

Dad didn't know why, but that was the first time he felt true unhappiness in his heart, and in his brain, he knew that something bad was happening in his world that he had no control over, and it weighed a lot on his mind. That heaviness stayed with him a long time. He later found that it was the same weight that his favorite cousin, Aunt Ruthie's daughter carried too. They both knew something. They were the same.

She and dad shared the same birthdate, and they were only a year apart in age. She and her three brothers were living back and forth between great grandmother's house and another Aunt's duplex in a slightly bigger town seventeen miles away. The last time dad saw any of the four cousins was right before school started.

"Big head," was what dad heard as he approached the screened porch of his grandma's old house. Dad grinned, *"who you calling "big head?"* As if timed perfectly, the three boys chorused, "big lip, bubba lip, big eyed potato chip." Dad ignored the pile on. His cousins were teasing, but they didn't mean to hurt his feelings. They just loved messing with him, and he was such a good sport about it externally. Inside, he felt

picked on sometimes, but he couldn't let on that he felt that way because his brothers and sisters had taught him to be tough. They always told him, *"never let them see you sweat or cry. Keep a poker face."*

He always tried to be tough. The test to be that way came when he saw Aunt Ruthie, her first day out of the hospital. He knew that his cousins were watching him, so he tried really hard not to cry. His best Aunt ever, didn't know him. She sat on the screened porch and stared out into who knows where. It was as if the person he saw before him was someone else, a stranger, someone from another part of space and time. The stranger was Aunt Ruthie's replacement. Dad was frightened of this person sitting inside of the screened porch.

As if on cue, his cousins asked him if he wanted to play hoops in the area behind the house, near the old automotive shop. They didn't seem to mind that she had changed. Happy to have her near them and their lives stable and somewhat normal again, they accepted that version of her without complaining, unconditionally. It was as if Uncle Charlie's DNA kicked in within each of them, signaling to Aunt Ruthie that she still mattered.

Although it didn't seem like it, the wheels inside of Aunt Ruthie's mind machine was still turning, her long-term memory was intact, and the short-term memory was getting better. Unbeknown to others, she was becoming well within her headspace, and wellness was spreading beyond her mental, to the physical parts of her being. It was the Uncle Charlie effect.

Somehow, she knew that he was still alive. Uncle Charlie was still missing, but nonetheless still alive. In her heart, she could feel him. Her brain's recorder played back over and over the good and the bad times that made their marital life together interesting and a constant adventure. Together, they were a force to be reckoned with. They loved and fought hard with each other, but loved more than anything else. Anyone could see it too. You never saw one without the other and if you did, you knew it was because of a work schedule or something important was keeping them apart, but only temporarily.

Uncle Charlie had a full-time job at the Sawmill and Aunt Ruthie worked part-time at the old folk care facility as a nurse's aide. Their work brought them a degree of satisfaction, but it was each other and the kids that made life into heaven on earth. Seeing them together made other people want to be married and have a family someday.

"They didn't have much, but they had each other," is what my dad would hear people say about them after Uncle Charlie left for Army basic training. No drill sergeant could wash Aunt Ruthie out of his brain. She stained his conscious, unconscious, and subconsciousness day, night, through push-ups and sit-ups, especially when his heartbeat was fastest and loudest as the breath of life carried him up and down the hilly landscape.

The squad could be heard over the walls of Fort Knox,
"Here we go again
Same old stuff again
Marching down the avenue
Few more days and we'll be though
I won't have to look at you
So, I'll be glad and so will you."
Uncle Charlie dreamt his favorite cadence,
"Hey, Hey Captain Jack
Meet me down
By the railroad track
With a bottle in your hand

I'm gonna be a drinking man
A drinking man
Hey, Hey Captain Jack
Meet me down
By the railroad track
With a K-bar in your hand
I'm gonna be a stabbing man
A stabbing man
A drinking man
Hey, Hey Captain Jack
Meet me down
By the railroad track
With a bible in your hand
I'm gonna be a preaching man
A preaching man
A stabbing man
A drinking man
Hey, Hey Captain Jack
Meet me down
By the railroad track
With a lady in your hand
I'm gonna be a loving man
A loving man
A stabbing man
A drinking man
Hey, Hey Captain Jack
Meet me down by the railroad track
With a rifle in my hand
I'm gonna be a shoot n' man
A shoot n' man
A loving man

A preaching man
A stabbing man
A drinking man
Hey, Hey Captain Jack
Meet me down by the railroad track
With an e-tool in my hand
I'm gonna be a A killing man
A killing man
A shoot n' man
A loving man
A preaching man
A stabbing man
A drinking man"

  Uncle Charlie would tweak the words a little whenever he was ordered out front to lead the squad in cadence. *"I'm gonna be a praying man, a praying man, a healing man, a loving man, a preaching man, a hugging man, a healthy man."* The first time he did it, everyone looked at each other awkwardly, as if to say, *"what the?"* Uncle Charlie repeated his rendition of the cadence again with natural, strong, leadership, and as if his words were the right words and he was making a few corrections to the cadence version the others knew well. However, it didn't take long for the other trainees to fall in step to his leadership and version of the cadence. It didn't take long for the drill sergeant to recognise corporal material too. At the end of boot camp, Uncle Charlie was pinned as a newly ranked corporal. It meant a pay raise and additional responsibilities. Aunt Ruthie no longer working, the nation's economy experiencing unprecedent inflation, she and the kids could use the money to buy what they couldn't buy before, new underwear, shoes, and a few other essentials. Being a corporal also meant that Uncle Charlie would be sent to the frontline were the fighting was most fierce and active. It was during such a time that Uncle Charlie's squad was separated from the platoon. The squad leaned heavily on his ability to lead during the worst of times. He discovered that he really was a praying man, a healing man, a loving man, a preaching man, a hugging man, and a healthy man and being all these things to his squad would bring an injured Uncle Charlie home late in December 1976 and most of the other men to their families, about two years prior. Home was truly where his heart was, and he couldn't wait to see the welcoming smiles of his family, after experiencing few smiles in the past few months.

Dad and his favorite cousin, Keila, knew in both their hearts too that he was alive. Uncle Charlie lived to tell the story. When everyone kept saying something about him being missing, Dad and Keila felt so much confusion. In their hearts, they knew it wasn't true. It was a mistake. Uncle Charlie wasn't missing from the whole Army, but it was true that he was missing from his unit, and he was missing his family and they were missing him too. It was also true that he and most of his squad fell in step with another unit that found them half starved, but surviving, using basic training tactics, and praying to Uncle Charlie's God. Their training and praying would help them see their friends and family again.

Years later, as if it was yesterday, Uncle Charlie could remember clearly feeling the touch or brush across his uncovered skin, the breeze in the air that gave wings to a small whisper in the airtight space of the C-7 Caribou. *"She's waiting for you."* Half awake, yet wide-eyed, he looked around, but no other eyes met his gaze. Sawing logs and other unusual sounds testified of the unknowing shared between the other flight passengers. No one else heard the sentence nor the urgency in its announcement and declaration that interrupted his state of deep meditation. Turning his head downward, he caught sight of the camouflaged banded time piece bound to his right wrist. It was three p.m. central time. Scheduled to land at the Military Airport before 5 o'clock traffic, his mind contained various thoughts that competed for his attention.

Things would be different and yet the same. Thoughts that were most important were those of his family welfare. It had been a long time since he received a letter from Ruthie, and she didn't seem herself in the last one sent a few weeks back. "Buck Sergeant, your bags." As the voice registered in his head, at the same time, he could feel a sharp pain that jarred him enough that he was stirred out of his daydream. He looked around slowly, he had forgotten his duffle bags and that he had received a field promotion two weeks ago. Still waiting for Uncle Charlie to respond, the tall man wearing six stripes on both upper arms of his military shirts, raised his voice slightly, eyes narrowing. *"Would you like for me to carry your bags for you? I accept tips too."* Uncle Charlie laughed, *"no sergeant, that won't be necessary,"* grabbed his bags and moved with purpose towards the white sign with blue letters that spelled bus. After securing his belongings in the lower compartment, he hiked up the stairs, nodded to the driver, who smiled back and said, *"welcome back, thank you for your service."* Under his breath, Uncle Charlie remarked, *"good to be back, thanks."* Settling in the back of the bus, he was soon fast asleep.

The seven-hour bus ride seemed like a few minutes. When he opened his eyes, the bus was half empty. As if on cue, the other passengers had quietly moved towards the entrance, not to disturb the brave man in uniform, who had fought for democracy and freedom. Fully awake and rested, Uncle Charlie marched quickly down the aisle, bringing up the rear of the other passengers. Exiting the greyhound, he looked around as if on a mission of reconnaissance. Comforted to ascertain the absence of an enemy, with one duffle bag packed on his back and the other in hand, he started towards his destination. After only a few steps forward he heard someone call to him, using his nick name, *"Big Boy."* It had been a long time since he was called that. Recognizing the voice, he smiled wide, turned around to find a friendly face in the trailing 1966 blue caprice. *"Get in Big Boy."* The four miles to 518 Nth. Forest Street, was filled with joyful laughter, reminiscing of over a decade back when both men were younger with dreams of grandiose. Both had planned to attend college as big-time athletes and then play football professionally. They knew for sure that their sons would follow in their footsteps, putting their small town on the map for other than notoriety.

As the caprice pulled in front of the house, the laughter slowly died down. The quiet soon filled the space between them. Uncle Charlie's friend grinned one last time while putting his hand face up, *"give me some skin Big Boy."* There was a slap of hand to hand, the lifelines of each meeting and then the same action on the backhand side. It was the secret shake of two childhood friends. In unison, they said, *"ok, man, see you,"* as the passenger side car door opened and closed. One last nod was given as Uncle Charlie retrieved the two duffle bags and closed the back passenger side door. The car sped off. The hedges next to the street still looked the same, but could use some trimming. The house could use a fresh coat of paint too. A honey-do list was appearing in his mind.

The wooden screen door was a sight for sore eyes, it was

familiar, the same as it was before his Army basic training and a tour in the unpopular war. He never liked the spooky, creepy sound the door made every time it swung wide open, but today, he welcomed it as sweet music to his ringing ears, one lending to a few disabilities that followed and were as visible as the medals pinned to his sharp dress blue uniform. Stepping through the old doorway with purpose, eyeing every detail of the small space, through his peripheral vision, he saw her. In the corner, Aunt Ruthie sat, still staring ahead as if looking past state borders, over the ocean, into the jungles of Vietnam. As if on cue, her raspy voice could be heard as the kids, including my dad were coming from the backyard and in the kitchen, where her nurse friend had just finished cooking dinner for the family. *"You are my God-sent husband."* Getting louder each time and by the third time, her voice rose as she elevated from sitting to standing. *"You are my God-sent husband!!!"*

    In earshot, my great-grandmother, and Aunt Ruthie's nurse friend raised their thin eyebrows, shrugged each shoulder, before deciding to rush towards the porch. Both weren't sure if Aunt Ruthie would be alone or overcome with signs of delusion. Within themselves they prayed for what they thought would be the best outcome, an old letter written in number two pencil lead from Uncle Charlie in Aunt Ruthie's hands or at least a touching scene of her holding a crumpled black and white photo of him. To their amazement, instead, it was him in the flesh that towered before Aunt Ruthie, his frame collapsing onto her smaller one, they were in full embrace, affection dripping from both their auras. Each was a gift to the other and the blessing that they both had prayed for.

Chapter Two

Uncle Charlie's return made that Christmas the most memorable for the family and neighbourhood. There was special warmth and cheer in the air, and a sense of Thanksgiving. With some of his combat pay, Uncle Charlie bought his four children and my dad, JT gifts that neither of them would have gotten because there wouldn't have been enough money to buy such extravagant presents usually. His only daughter, Keila, a daddy's girl received a most precious gold chain with a locket shaped like a cross attached. Inside the cross was filled with red dye. The Anniversary week marking the end of the unpopular war, a few days before Easter, the red liquid outlined the outer edges of the beautiful metal case and its gold colour seemed brighter.

Green, the colour of the envy experienced by my dad's male cousins who wanted his gift, but it was also symbolic of spring and the gift that brightened my dad's day, reminding him that winter was only temporary, like his mom's illness. Green apple was what my dad called his awesome brand-new bicycle with its big black rubbery spoked wheels. Training wheels attached, built to roll stealthily across the almost blindingly white snow-blanketed ground that lay outside the doors of his family's modest three bedroom Jim Walter home.

Imaginative and too young to be cognizant of the weighted heaviness everyone that loved his mum shared on that wonderful, memorable Christmas morning, life was good. It seemed obvious to any on-looker peering from the outside of his world that he was shielded from the cold reality of his mother's worsening condition as his long legs pedaled that new trike. If in vintage condition that shiny beauty could fetch a pretty penny in today's market as a known classic vehicle. Dad often talked about it as the best gift ever. He beamed with pride and ready to show off his treasured pedal-driven cycle, dad sped into grandfather and Etta's sleeping quarters where she lay recovering from another bad recurring episode of the illness with its flu and pneumonia-like symptoms that gripped her very existence with the intention of taking the life that she so intently held onto with all of her being, it was a daily duel between a honourable life and death's dark forces, the war raging within. She breathed every breath as if each was a gift and felt a sense of urgency as she watched her baby boy ride back and forth and in, around and out and back into her private space, sharing the rich oxygenated air with her youthful, but poor, frail frame. Every breath was precious, she knew it, but dad would only discover its worth in his late adult years.

Etta's illness was hard on him. On the days she slept more than usual, he would walk over to his grandma's house to see Aunt Ruthie, who, now that Uncle Charlie was back, was well, the madness beaten back became one of his main caretakers. Some days, he would stand at Etta's bedroom door before knocking and allow his tears to run down his smooth, red checks, some of the salty liquid seeping into the corners of his quivering mouth.

For years, he struggled with occasional bouts of guilt and depression, the madness not completely overtaking him. He blamed himself for her suffering. If he wasn't conceived…………….. *"If I could go back in time,"* he once said out loud. Wrapping his mind around morbid thoughts, turning them round and round in his brain, each time he grew more emotionally paralysed from the heart up, breathing alternating quick, sharp, shallow then much slower deep breaths as the memory played of his mother, preparing to sacrifice her own life for his own. Laying on her bed, its old, rusted iron frame creaked with the slightest movement or shifting of weight. It was as if someone was cruelly pressing the rewind button of some video equipment over and over without editing any scenes each time, leaving in the graphic horror. In need of emotional rehabilitation, he hardened until even his heart grew as stiff and stony as his rigid thinking. Should he question his mother's Maker? She was a person of faith. Trembling, he stopped short of blasphemy. Answers would come soon enough he assured himself. Shifting in his mind and heart from anger to guilt and then back to anger was emotionally and physically tiring. He was just a little kid he told himself each time he struggled with the seesawing of deep sadness and guilt, hoping to win this time and cause the balance to remain in the middle so that neither overwhelmingly deeply sad emotion nor guilt becomes the victor; knowing full-well that If he wasn't careful with the wielding of precious thoughts that he could easily become convinced that it was his fault and darkness would take a firm hold of him once the scale tipped to one side. Second moms and stepmoms could substitute, but never replace a first mom. There seemed to be no pity for the weary soul of a creature needing caring for, a lad in that school-age developmental stage who longed to free himself of the misery of having to relive a time that should be forgotten, suppressed even or should it? Dark thoughts many times would almost overcome his sensibility throughout the early years of life, but a will to survive usually won out thanks be to the maker of heaven and earth. If dad heard me say the latter, he would have said, *"who, the maker of what and what?* Then, I would have said, *"the maker of you, me, and the whole world."* Although I never knew her, I'm told that I'm like my grandma Etta, a person of faith too. Admittedly, I'm a little worried that maybe dad doesn't believe in a higher power anymore.

I worry too about the morbid stuff he sometimes repeats, like his mum was healthy when the bundle of joy, my uncle, born two years before him came along. He used to say that he would bet any amount that she was happier before her accident, his birth. Sadly, his brothers and cousins use to joke and wear out the same ole tired line over and over that he was a test-tube baby or that he wasn't Grandpop's child because he seemed different in some way. Not sure what to believe, in his little mind he leaned towards the notion that he wasn't supposed to be born and therefore he had no purpose for being alive and battled with this inclination for years. The one question that remained foremost for a long time in his mind was whether he was conceived first in the minds of the two people he called mum and dad before the deed was done. Was his birth planned or not? And he wondered for a little while as a child if they thought to give him away or terminate him. Too late to wish him back into the Creator's thought and furthermore out of his plan for her life, he was here waiting to be cared for by Etta and yet she couldn't any longer be responsible for his wellbeing.

49-year-old Etta lay on her sick bed watching him study her, unable to speak, she wished they both knew sign language or morse code. Speaking instead, using the international language, love was communicated between them. Children born to older parents come into the world with a certain something within their being that adds to their intelligence and makes them either a little less or more than average. He hoped that he possessed the latter of the two because his brothers teased him for not seemingly knowing as much as they did and always said that he sounded like the cartoon character, Baby Huey whenever he was upset. They were astonished when they found out that he was what superstitious people called a Knower. Few people believed and beloved what those people imagined to be true, but as recollected by Aunt Ruthie, Grandma Etta did and couldn't help, but think deeply about what they said about her baby boy, JT She knew that there was some truth to what they remarked about him and though his big sisters and Aunt Ruthie were his caretakers, she still worried about who would guide him if she was taken from him. No one could do it as well as she could. Her little dude was remarkable, but also mischievous.

    Before losing her voice a few weeks ago, while watching her observe him, he noticed with delight the pretty, deep red plums that sat waiting to be polished and quickly ravished on her bedside table. Grandma Etta saw him eying the forbidden sweet fruit that belonged only to her. Grandpop, her prince since they were young, loved showering her with gifts, had brought the delicious treat by during his lunch hour and warned the children of its value and assured them of a painful punishment if they even dreamt of taking their fill of any of them without his bride's permission. My dad, JT had a daring plan to make his move towards my grandmother's bedside; hoping that his manners and charm would be that of a trained professional. Etta, named after a daytime T.V. soap opera star knew an actor when she saw one, trained her eyes to her baby boy's movements. Catching sight of his face with its bashful smile, deep dimples, and spell-binding big brown eyes, she smiled at the miracle child and gave a nod of approval for him to continue pretending he was only there to spend time with her with no hidden motives. Before long, smoothly, JT quickly took full advantage of her generosity to be present with her. She was under his spell; resistance was simply futile. He was as greedy as any healthy, energetic, and growing boy; without hesitation and shame he grabbed the delicious fruit without being given permission to do so. Sticking one in his mouth while hiding the other three within his favorite baseball cap, he quickly kissed his mom, intending to make a quick get-a-way. Etta frowned with disapproval. It hurt her to have to scold such a sweet face, but it was her duty to nurture, protect him from a stomachache and to teach him good manners. While scowling, in a less than kind voice she said, *"put one of those plums back. Your big eyes are too greedy for your own good."* Like the spoil brat he was, he stomped off towards the door improperly; not realizing that Grandpop had not yet left for the second half of his workday. As Grandpop with his bulging muscles and no non-sense attitude walked through the narrow hallway, still in earshot, as his little boy grumbled some colourful language learned somewhere outside of his good, wholesome upbringing. Within what seemed microseconds the whole neighbourhood could hear my grandmother yell for my Grandpop and my dad knew what that meant. My Grandpop was the enforcer of rules and dad had just broken one. The strong patriarch was judge and jury. It's safe to assume that it was a while before that youngster used profanity again.

 Etta died six months later, one month after dad's birthday. Later when me and my sister were born dad conversed often about how crucial it was to have both parents around at their child's early birthdays. Each year, instead of having an awesome, memorable birthday social gathering for himself, he chose not to celebrate. The gruesome memory of his mother's death and a religious funeral event given in her honour and often referred to as her home-going, left an indelible impression on him.

Not dissimilar to birthday parties, the after funeral gathering, a death-day party, seemed just another observant religious gathering to dad and an excuse for love-ones and strangers alike to over-indulge in a banquet table of greens, cornbread, homemade rolls, turkey and dressing, sweet potato pie, pound cake included in a menu full of other delicious items and a punch that included an unhealthy red artificial coloured cool-aid and 7-up mixture with sliced lemons floating on top of half-melted ice cubes. Assigned to a picnic table next to the corner of my great grandma's house and a huge tree with the other kids, his brothers, sisters, and cousins included, he sat staring into space, an alternate universe maybe, possibly a multiverse. His consciousness seemed a weird headspace that day. Both aware of self and what seemed like more than one reality, he questioned the clarity of all that existed in those few hours around him.

It all seemed part of a vivid dream, it had not fully become reality and seemed to be part of a development of his imagination, the gradual focus that his mother lay before him at the wake, then funeral, and later grave site, breathless among a list of attendees that he had not invited to share with him this moment in time that he selfishly made all about him. Yet they sat with him in a place that housed for this precious suspension of time, a space loaned to him and Etta so that they may have just a moment together to be, to exist without watches and clocks measuring out seconds, minutes, and hours in their last day of temporal gazing and meditation. As dad stared downward at the grave site, taking in the treasures of breath and silence, it happened the second time in one day. A voice, slightly above a whisper, sounded out in clear syllables and vowels, the word, *"goodbye."* At that moment, although startled by what he heard, it was made clear to him that he and she were not going to breathe or share the same air again, let alone have dialogue.

The first time he heard her voice, it was at the funeral, and he wasn't sure what to make of it or if anyone else heard it too, so he studied his surroundings for paranormal activity and watched people for signs of affirmation in his knowing and confirmation that hearing the voice happened. The encouragement and testimony didn't occur until years later that his sanity was intact, and his eardrums were receiving unusually heightened soundwaves on that day. In the meantime, his inner life continued to experience activity unknown to none-Knowers. Looking across the room he witnessed another happening near the dilapidated picture frame next to an antique mirror that Etta called the looking glass, the word he had heard twice in the day was spelled in bold black letters, *"GOODBYE,"* and was surrounded and shrouded in the brightest light that he had ever seen. He remembered seeing the same light in his mother's coffin. She lay cloaked in it, her clothes barely visible.

In front, closest to the coffin, sitting on his big sister's lap while his brother, who was two years older than him sat on their oldest sister's lap, he made an observation of the event that was taking place around him. While long, drooping faces painted with mascara played their role in the funeral drama, cultural music snaked its way over, around pews, and into saddened hearts, the drama and funeral director who was also the preacher waited his turn to do one of the most important things his training prepared him to do. He had rehearsed his multiple parts and was well prepared to do what the family was accustomed to and according to the custom of the audience and more particularly or specifically, meet the demands of the critics who trained their eyes on him as if on a mission of surveillance. He certainly would give them all what they wanted, needed, and throw in a few surprises too. In dad's eyes, the preacher seemed to be a talented professional, and had a similarity to a trained racehorse. Once out of the gate he would give his best performance to all who looked on from their seats. Bets were placed on the preacher to do well, and others watched closely for stumbles out of the gate. His loss would be their gain. Confidence could be his jockey and it appeared to be so. Seemingly, the family had chosen the right representative of humankind to express the sentiment of a remarkable and precious lost to all the world, a credit to the gene pool.

His heart showed a different creature, God's creature created for his service. This creature struggled with all sorts of insecurity. If dad knew then how to, he would have prayed for him, but he had not learned sincere, personal prayer yet. Prayer learned early on in his Christian sect or denomination seemed more religious than something born out of spiritual attunement. They prayed more like unknowing and unlinked pious folk that were unsure of the part they played in the world and knew even less about an all-powerful, omniscient, omnipresent Being that was caretaker of creation and spiritual navigational system for the lost. To triumph over anxiety, the preacher began a prayer in his heart while the soloist sang Amazing Grace. He knew that he was next on the programme bulletin. In dad's community, a preacher's reputation as a renowned speaker could be upheld and extended if he proved himself in the funeral arena. Unlike other religious events and humanity's sacred moments, the end of temporal life activities was both festive and sad, but most of all extremely emotionally exhausting.

While dad's family was putting heads, faces, necks, chests, arms, butts, legs, and feet in their funeral garb the preacher was gargling, and humming. His voice had to be finely tuned before he could ready the rest of himself for the engagement that lay before him. Stretched to the brink of breaking, his mind shifted from tuning to getting Etta's soul from earth to heaven and then directing the living from a hellish lifestyle to one that would afford their souls the privilege of joining her in a new heavenly home. *"How would he orchestrate such a feat in the minutes given him,"* the preacher thought.

While our family waited for everyone to gather at the funeral parlor so that all may be given careful instructions about the epic trek by foot from the old church to the donated cemetery plot, the preacher knelt at the mourning bench, hoping that God would hear what he moaned and groaned before Him. Meanwhile, neither the preacher nor the family members realised that they were all being watched under a microscope.

Far above in imagination, watching from his sister's lap those who appeared as small as microbes, in a place, a chapel that seemed to him like a regular house because it had the same feel as his earthly father's house, but dad couldn't help wondering what heavenly Father God's house would really be like, the place where his mum was said to go after the final exhale and hearing the trumpet sound for the dead who believed God exist and would come for them. Not sure if he believed the stories of Sunday School, he was still waiting to experience the faith that a place existed that would be what people warmly referred to as the place where everyone feels like family and one where they would all get together in a special place where all the houses were mansions. In the meantime, he longed for the experience of familiarity and warmth of kinship on earth as it would be in heaven. At that time, he did not feel that Etta and Grandpop's church family was his family. He imagined that any family that he was tied to should be a freely giving functional one. Seemingly misunderstood by that family, the religious hypocrites that had filled the pews of the chapel most of the time, he felt utter mental affliction and oppression. Whether gift or curse, he knew things that children usually overlooked, and grownups hoped to keep secret. He knew people and what they were capable of, positive or negative. It was hard to hide from him the things that a person did not want revealed about themselves.

Seemingly naïve, he spent most of his life hoping that evil was good struggling like the creature in the cocoon to show its true nature. Through the years, he would see the true nature, the heart of a person and chose not to believe what he was chosen to see because of his immaturity and fear that the revelation would somehow change him or affect him negatively. Through an unknown power he could see the secret things as clearly as an adult later in life as he could as a young boy only wanting to be normal. Was he born for this; to see the horror, guilt, tragedy, and pain that filled the lives of so many? Whether it was in his mother's womb or on his sister's lap something took place in history. A little small-town boy who seemed destined to repeat the cycle of past lifers was chosen to carry the burden that ladened a small slender frame and without intentionally trying to, changed the lives of countless lost souls that met him. Yet a haunting question stayed as much with him as the burden.

"And my mum died for……?"

JT had heard people say, *"as one comes in another soul leaves this earth."* He questioned their superstition as he pondered the necessity of the exchanging of a new life for an old one. Still, not sure what really caused his mum to become so ill and eventually die, he blamed his untimely advent into their world. Puzzled by the significance of him being given life and her young life being shortened in comparison to her mother's life, who lived to be 100 years old on earth, left him with disturbing feelings that would plague him for most of his life. In time, as he grew older and more curious, the little boy that stayed with him, full of questions that needed answers, wished to inquire further, but at the same time was afraid to. He was taught not to question God. Then he thought to himself that *"maybe it wasn't God's will after all."* Dad's family were of the working poor and their hourly pay was barely enough to pay the bills. Extra money to start savings and emergency accounts was only a dream. It was public knowledge that hospitals were operated with the assistance of the government, but required that an unaffordable percentage of hospital bills be paid via from the checking and savings of the victims of degenerative physical bodily conditions. Grandpop and Grandma Etta had worked for their employers full-time for over twenty years and received medical benefits that could help with some of the hospital and medication cost, but they needed the co-pay amount. Aunt Ruthie and Uncle Charlie were working full time again and could help with some of the medication cost and made sure dad was taken care of too. To see a specialist; one that would know exactly how to treat Etta's illness in time to extend her life to at least her mother's current age, could only be hoped for. Soon they would have to decide whether to leave

Etta into the hands of fate or her faith, searching desperately for anyone that would loan their family money to see a medical specialist or give to the prophet/prophetess that believed Etta could be miraculously healed. The money never came, but something strange happened. One morning Etta awoke early to a strange peace. It was as for the first time in a long time she had clarity. She knew what was coming next and all the things that needed to be done. There was much preparation and she needed to talk about it and share something very important with Aunt Ruthie, her daughter Keila, and dad. Only they could be told the things that needed to be told and only they would Etta tell, because the Looking Glass had chosen those three and the futures of many other people depended on the steps and path taken by those three. It would be a mission that seemed impossible or with a little faith, the possible would happen.

Agents for change, they were, however, my Grandma Etta would always be known as the most remarkable one of the four. The others were not any less gifted, but lacked her toughness and insight. Grandpop could never truly keep up with her and he understood little of what she talked about even though she usually only spoke a few meaningful sentences at a time.

The morning of her clarity, a picture-perfect day, she spoke more words than he had heard her speak in a very long time. Her energy level was very high and her appetite for loving affection for and from Grandpop had returned and those were only a few surprises she had for him that day. Known for her angelic voice in her youth, it had returned as well. As she rose from her bed of affliction, watching Grandpop watch her with disbelief, she hummed a familiar tune while she pulled the fifty count sheets and twill blanket off her legs and swung both lower extremities and feet to the side of the mattress and frame. She nearly sent the vase and shriveled flowers on the bedside table tumbling to the cheap linoleum flooring as her feet met the smooth foundation and her hands and arms swung outward wildly and widely, assisting her eventual bearing. Grandpop rushed to her side, but stop short of grabbing her because she gave him a look that directed and instructed his steps and movement towards her. Smiling, Etta held out her right hand with palm turned down and Grandpop now closer pressing his left leg softly, but snuggly against her right thigh, he allowed her right hand to press downward onto his opened left palm. In sync as two telepaths, together, as always, they achieved another unthinkable task. As Grandpop rose to the occasion, Etta rose one last time from what many of her friends and family referred to as her deathbed, lifting her head and gazing forward her eyes met the three that she intended to summon to her presence.

Out in the narrow hallway, near the bedroom doorframe, all four stood with near perfect posture, waiting for what would come next. Etta moved slowly towards them at first and as if she was sure her gate had loosened and her legs were working properly again, her stride and pace quickened. There seemed a newfound freedom in her movement and mannerism. Along with the bounce in her step, her countenance beamed, the epiretinal membrane and rhytid had faded and both were unnoticeable, the youthful twinkle in her eyes had returned. An aura of joyfulness overwhelmed everyone nearby. Grandpop fell to his knees as if by instinct as his eyes filled with blurring tears that momentarily concealed his ability to see, sobbing uncontrollably, he later spoke of this experience as a sadly strange and at the same time moment of complete joy. His wife of nearly three decades turned to him, placed her hands on his head, cheeks and finally shoulder blades, and then spoke at a volume of sound that only Grandpop's ears could detect. Her comforting words profoundly affected the flow of his tears, they slowed to a drip every few seconds. Sniffling, he accepted her embrace and kiss and permitted her to turn to the others. Aunt Ruthie, first in line, her favorite sister-in-law, but more like a biological twin sister than any other, shied away at first and then as if on cue stepped forward to receive what seemed a farewell of sorts and simultaneously a gift and she would say years later, it was a blessing as well as a hand-off in the game or relay in the race of life. Aunt Ruthie was given the charge to stay the course and prepare the other two Knowers to take their place in the coming years. She nodded and stepped aside as Keila stepped cautiously forward. Respectfully, keeping her head and eyes downward until asked to look into her favorite auntie Etta's eyes, Keila felt her legs wobble and knees buckle. Etta's calves where near and Keila reached out for them. The muscles and skin were soft and warm. Etta waited for the right words and asked Keila to recite them. *"Stand for the truth and nothing else, the past reveals the future's quest."* Keila was helped to her feet and guided by Etta to the old Looking Glass that had belonged to the family for more than a century. Keila's journey through life in the present and future had a clarity that was distinctly revealed in past events. Uncle Charlie, Aunt Ruthie, her brothers, and her favorite cousin JT had and would continue to play important roles in her life's drama. Each action would have a reaction. Responses would carry consequences. The subsequent revelations would be precise. Keila looked at her mom, Aunt Ruthie and then at her Auntie Etta and then turned to her favorite cousin, who seemed to be in a trance. He had entered a state of knowing. Etta's baby boy JT, had seen this day coming and other days ahead of his own struggle with her eventual demise, but in the present moment he was swept up and away into a strangeness and indescribable state found between the conscious and subconscious.

Unusual thoughts, a heightened interest in illness, and death filled his young mind. In fact, melancholy thought almost practically consumed his psyche most of the time. JT believed his mother's death to be one of slow and horrible passing into temporal oblivion until judgement day. Her morbidity was more than our family could handle, but my dad, JT developed a complex. Each time, I cringed as I heard him say more than once *"why couldn't she have lived, and I died. Whatever message I'm supposed to carry she could have easily carried. My siblings needed her far more than they needed another mouth taking from their already shrinking portions of the daily, basic food groups. My dad needed his wife, the mother of the little people that looked to him for guidance, nurturing and strength. I took her from them when I came to exist. Existing like most parasites do; I used her until she was used up. Did she know what I was doing? Was it etched in her memory till the end? Could she have chosen to live? Like a camera, her memory at life's end was the film discharged or disconnected from the place its manufacturer had carved for it, only in its place to dwell for a period of time until it had achieved its purpose. Was my mother only supposed to be here for that period of time in which she was purposed? Did she achieve her maker's purpose for her and us? I can't help, but wonder."* The wondering led to his wandering well into his middle years. On his forty-ninth birthday, he cried almost incessantly as he thought about their last day together, which happened to be her forty-ninth year.

After Aunt Ruthie, Keila, and Grandpop were asked by Etta to allow her some time alone with her baby boy, the two of them walked slowly to the back screened in porch and down three cemented steps to soft green grass and a few sparse dandelions that seemed to be smiling up at mother and son. Although they had spent hours talking about what mattered to them, their time together seemed to be, but a few precious seconds. Time would encapsulate two or three memories of her and gift them in a neat package to him. Any other memories were mere fantasies and those borrowed from the immense collection of the consciousness of family and friends. In kindness and sometimes pity, their memories of her were embellished. In truth, no one person knew her well, but together their stories brought him closer to who she was and that comforted him each time he was held captive in a room of one or more people who served his need to know again or to know more and fill a hole in his heart and the mindful hunger that was insatiable. He was willing to travel through the airway, on trailways, and highways for an old and forgotten or seemingly new story because he had to know.

Year forty-nine was hard for him. It was the year he stopped speaking most words unless they were meaningful to others who needed to know. When he spoke, others would listen intently, waiting for something else, hoping to walk with JT and help him move past complexity to simply understanding the meaning of all his experiences. A profoundness enveloped his whole demeaner. The company he kept was intentionally sought. No one spoke, but everyone wanted his train of thought to pull into the station to remain still for servicing at some point before moving quickly along, stimulated, as evidenced by the higher synaptic counts and unusual emotional outbursts.

Everyone was caught off guard by the unexpected seesawing of laughter to tears and what appeared to be incessant joy and then grief for what seemed long periods because JT usually kept his bearing well. He was known to be private and most of the time unusually stoic. To witness an unusual, uncharacteristic emotional rollercoaster displayed by him outwardly was more than they could have prepared for. That year would be forever deposited and catalogued in the memory banks of every person present.

The lessons learned would be passed down to future generations of Knowers who continued to exist only if their family's heirloom existed, similar to my dad JT's dilapidated mirror, the looking glass, one that had been removed from plain sight and hidden, to be revealed when it was needed most. Until it's hiding place could and would be revealed, JT continued collecting memories that were the breadcrumbs to truth-telling, the bedrock of knowing. Often thinking what would Etta do, he stayed the course, notwithstanding the present and future struggles influenced by the past and genetics.

Chapter Three

Dad didn't remember Etta very well. He just remembered certain details of moments spent with her like the one of their last Christmas together, or the day she died, and the way she looked lying in the casket. I guess one can say he had flashbacks. They're like snap shots taken of the brief moments that she and he had together. He thought that perhaps some part of him died with her; that part of him that is supposed to connect him with his mate. His relationships with the prior candidates for marriage were usually short ones and the one with my mum lasted the longest. Supporting him during the darkest moments of his life, through the rants and raves, ups and downs, as he rode the emotional rollercoaster was worn by her as a badge of honour. Loving dad unconditionally, my mum remained strong during the times where many wives would have abandoned him. Her husband's struggle was born and travailed through childhood and adult terrorism. PTSD remained as evidence of what would be a lifelong war waged. Harmed emotions, psyche, and physical were inclusive of its effects throughout his youth and well into middle age.

While together, a year or two beyond the newly wed period, it was hard for her to sleep beside him when he cried and yelled epithets into the darkness while sitting in bed half asleep and half tranced, arms flinging wildly in front and over his head, and then punching the air and the invisible demon in front of him. On those nights she prayed that God would intervene because in the dark virtual reality she could not help him.

While she prayed outside of the reality he experienced, he wrestled violently inside a realm of what seemed impossible, but existed and could be only seen by Knowers. It was something that she was being protected from. When he awoke the next morning to see her laying on the floor shaking uncontrollably, he pitied her. She had the misfortune of marrying him and keeping his secrets. Kneeling beside her, he whispered, *"my love, I am sorry. It will be better someday for you, I promise, you'll see."* Placing his hands on the small of her back, then softly rubbing in circular motions. He hummed a few lines of her favorite song. When she turned over onto her back, he saw the smile that always made him feel warm in a heart that was most of the time cold. *"Girl, I would drink yo bath water."* It was what she needed to hear, kind of like a code phrase that he had come back to her. Punching him in the chest and then laughing, they both laid on their backs at the same time. Tears streaming from the smokey corner of her eyes she spoke in a half-joking and half-serious tone of voice, *"You better drink my bath water boy."* Both then busted out laughing at the same time. Their relationship was like Grandpop and Etta's. They knew each other so well and had each other's back. She was his ride or die, he often thought. Without looking at him directly in the eyes, she said, *"you really scared me this time. Man, I didn't think you were coming back this time.* Pausing, as if waiting for a response and half hoping that he would say something to put her at ease, but there was only the silence that lay between them. *Did you hear what I said? Where you at dude? I don't know how much I can take of this.* Without thinking first before speaking, she said what was in heart out loud, *"Your dad was right. You are different. I guess if he could love ya mama, I can love you.* She quickly put both hands over her mouth. *JT, I'm sorry. I shouldn't have said that. I didn't mean that anything was wrong with her or that anything is wrong with you, I, I, I....*was the last thing that JT heard her stammer before tuning out the explanation attempted and honesty on display. Remembering his dad's last words before leaving his small town behind, he knew that his wife was right, and he knew that she wasn't trying to hurt him with speaking truth to him. Besides, Etta, Aunt Ruthie, and his big sisters expected him to be tough enough to take a little straight talk. He had a good woman, and he knew it. Admittedly, it was still hard to hear her say the words that stung like green alcohol on a fresh open womb. A voice somewhere around them added to the conversation he was having inside of his head, *"man-up, you need thicker skin, don't be a punk."*

Looking around the room, he felt he was under surveillance. Meanwhile, his wife, my mother, was still trying to get his attention and apologise for the earlier gaffe. As she went on to say, *"blah, blah, blah,"* he rolled over to his stomach and crawled to the bedframe, placing his head underneath to look for the place the voice came from. At first, he thought he saw two eyes looking back at him, blinking once. Closing his eyes and then slowly opening them again, nothing was there, no sound was made. Agitation started setting inward.

As the warring inside continued, he found himself in a fetal position. He felt defeat approaching and wanted to lay down his pitiful weapons, used to fight the madness that would try taking charge of his thought process. Not wanting to fight anymore it was easy for him to give in and become hardened, distress, and changed; it was easy for him to say, *"I am who I am, product of my environment, culture, and cognitive imperfections,"* every time he felt the wind being knocked out of him. But he realised that he had to speak words that were truer of his nature, words that define who he really was, is, and will be in the end. The wife of his youth, one of the few who knew JT's secret, his ending, the truth owned by Etta's baby boy, and the weighted revelation of that knowledge was heavy, pitted within his gut. He had told her that someday the sails of revelation would catch the wind and the vessel of knowledge would be pushed and pulled to the seemingly distant shores of ticking time and uncharted destinations. She didn't understand at first, but then one day it became clear to her that he was that vessel.

Often searching for answers; there were times when he felt the need for a mind and heart deep dive. His emotions at times got the best of him. Eyes red, frequent late morning rising and shaking uncontrollably, he finally made an appointment with a therapist. Dad confided, *"I'm in trouble and I need your help. I'm haunted by something or someone or more than one. It's hard to explain, but I'll keep trying. Let me know if you feel me."* Some of what he said made sense while other parts of what he said didn't make any sense at all. That therapist tried really hard to hear and understand as best as anyone who heard about disturbing experiences, voices, and images could understand. At the end of the session, what was truly apparent was that he was in need of mental and emotional healing at least. The therapist finished writing on her notepad and then handed him a prescription for delusion, hallucinations, illusions, disordered thinking and behavior, agitation, inappropriate reactions, phobia, lack of pleasure or interest in activities, lack of motivation to do anything and decreased speech output. His next appointment was scheduled, and she reached out to shake his hand, intending to rush him out of the door.

After JT was out the door, she closed it softly behind her. Rubbing the back of her neck, she shook her head and placed the palm of her hands on her cheeks as she thought out loud how exhausted she felt from JT's presence and rapid speaking. It was as if she felt what he thought was his family's heavy burden of keeping an eye on him. She had taken him on as a patient because she loved his Aunt Ruthie and Uncle Charlie.

They called her their miracle worker. Both Aunt Ruthie and Uncle Charlie as perfect as they were for each other had their own personal baggage before their marriage and collected more once blissfully together forever, for better or worse. Tested by Aunt Ruthie's sister, Molly's death and Uncle Charlie's wartime adventures they were survivors of eventful dark moments, but not completely overcomers of dark forces and were barely thrivers in their own right and were grateful to be led to Fealgud Marshall, MD, PHD at the VA Medical Centre, a compassionate friend of lost souls and hard cases. Ruthie and Charlie had hoped that she could work a similar miracle in JT's life.

She canceled her other appointments for the day because her exhaustion grew as she thought about how JT seemed engulfed with agony as he talked of his mother and big sisters who greatly impacted his interaction with his wife and daughters. In short, he was a mess, and no one seemed to know why and how it happened. He lived in a real world where everyone had ears that were plugged with their own immediate cares, a husband, children, career, mounting bills, personal scars, and unwanted memories. So, it was no wonder that when he pleaded for help to gain a sense of sanity back, he was ignored. His family was frustrated with him because he had not learned to thrive. Survival would only get him so far. The therapist had questioned whether everyone he loved affirmed each other's fears that maybe hospitalization would be needed at some point. She had asked him how he felt about that. JT joked that he didn't know if the world could handle him being away. Laughter was used to guard his true feelings on any serious matter. Inside, he knew that the day would come when he would have to seriously consider what they feared may happen. Other Knowers in their family were overcome and it was the one thing that Etta had asked God, and Aunt Ruthie for help with. She had prayed to the unseen One and pleaded with her favorite sister-in-law to not abandon JT

Aunt Ruthie and his favorite cousin Keila understood him more than most and helped him walk life's mental health tight rope well into his late twenties. Keila's path was different from his. Off the grid, she had not been located in years and if he could see her again, he thought, *"in me, there would be balance again."*

Dr Marshall had listened intently while making notes of dad's comments, questions, and his seemingly irrational state of mind. The psychiatrist was particularly interested in dad and Grandpop's relationship. JT remarked that *"I made little sense to a father who knew little about who I was and would become. I think he was more familiar with my shadow self and the healthy condition of my physicality than my personality, inner abilities, hopes, dreams, inner most thoughts and being. He didn't know me any more than I knew him. I was another mouth to feed, another youngling to bring up in his image and more important in the image of the Creator of all humankind. To him, that was truth and truth set him free from seeing more than that. Maybe not just truth, but perhaps, the distress and weariness of being a single parent for awhile had quite a bit to do with it as well. My siblings and I have gone over this truth many times together and pondered it within alone, trying to analyse and make sense of it. Daddy had taught us a funny, hard kind of love. It was a love like no other that we knew of. We learned patience, long-suffering, and forgiveness without conditions. However, with that lesson came a price tag. Bitterness and resentment burrowed deep within our selves like a nocturnal animal waiting to show itself once a cloak of darkness covers the surface of mother earth, hiding and shielding it from those that opposed its existence. My siblings and I knew that we had a dark side that opposed the very good that our mother wanted to preserve and that our father would spend most of his life pounding into us what he thought was good for us whether we liked it or grew to hate it. Confused and dazed while still trying to make sense of our father's logic and way of doing things, we grew little by little more and more disillusioned; not knowing whether we were submitting to the good of God or the strong-will of a God-fearing man, we questioned it to our wits end. Like our father, we took on a weariness of our own. Before long, we truly became our father's spawn, and our truth became the truth of a strong-willed man and occasional drill sergeant. Some of us learned perseverance while other siblings broke under pressure and never saw their full potential. Either way there was much suffering under the weight of defeat, agony, and the occasional physical and psychological heavy hand of a burdened single parent. I could not help, but wonder; would this animosity and almost, borderline disdain for life and disappointment in one of those that made my life possible exist if my mother's young life had not been snatched like a purse full of valuables?"* As if collecting his thoughts while keeping his emotions in check, dad swallowed before continuing. The therapist handed him a box of soft tissues and encouraged him to set his feelings free. After sobbing for what seemed to him longer than the allotted appointed time, he continued with what was in his heart.

"As I struggled to be an innocent knower, life without my mum grew more difficult to live in the ordinary way. Living in a world of fantasy and imagination became the norm and a safe place to hide while all the bad stuff past me by or had its way with me, which ever God allowed to happen and in what ever order they were allowed to happen. Rapidly growing psychologically harmed and stoic as I matured, middle school education in the Independent School District and the streets ushered in the unexpected experiences, usually welcomed by older kids. Memories of learning the ugliness and beauty of life in the classrooms and neighbourhoods of our small town competed with the flashbacks of my mother's illness, and death and my father's struggle to be mother, father, and provider. Most times I try to blot out the bad memories with more pleasant childhood memories like walking with my friends to Mr James Boston's store to buy soda pops, Corn Nuts, Red Kool-Aid, Penny cookies, and Penny candy, and seeing young girls getting their hair straightened with hot combs on their grandmother's porch, and cool older boys strutting down the street with fresh oily afros dripping on their skulls, and the hot summer nights that were made even more unbearable with mosquitoes on the prowl like vampires that hunted day and night. And I remember seeing a hilarious, crazy dude called Naked Man for obvious reasons roam the streets all day everyday and finally be picked up by one of the town's authority and upholders of the law for indecent exposure, and Jr. King,

the town idiot said the silliest things, while the town's philosopher debated the silly notion whether or not a man actually went to the moon. Meanwhile, Aunt Mae Mae and her boyfriend sat smoking on the porch and drinking drinks not for kids who should be minding their business. And I remember late nights bringing early risings, and summer jobs to buy school clothes, and building two small tents out of bed sheets big enough for one person to fit under each. I was not given permission to use those sheets and would probably be severely punished later. I remember boys teasing girls and girls teasing boys and walking to the park where the swing sets were unsafe for anyone that weighed more than 70lbs. I loved going to the park with my friends, but hated to meet any rival, bad-parented children of whatever age. They always started trouble with us or with loners who chose isolation over socialization. It was good to have friends. I could not imagine life without human companionship. I like meeting and talking to people." The psychiatrist interjected with some questions and asked for an example of an adult that JT enjoyed conversing with and whom he trusted with his most inner thoughts. Dad picked up the dialogue at the point of the interruption as easily as his stream of consciousness would allow.

"One day as I sat swinging, I thought about my favorite kindergarten teacher, Ms Kindleson. She was a sweet plump and pleasant soul who I thought knew everything about anything. I imagined us discussing the beanstalk story. This was a rebuttal to the story of Jack and the Beanstalk. Being a thoughtful little boy and at times responsive to the troubles of others I said to Ms Kindleson, 'What if the giant was really a good guy who respected others and their property and only asked the same in return.' She replied, 'What do you mean sweetie?' I returned with, 'What if the story of Jack and the Beanstalk was told differently.' As she looked at me with a curious look, she asked me to tell the story the way I thought it should be told. So, I started telling the giant's side of the story. His version of events that happened was a refute of Jack's story; the boy who stole from him and got away with the crime."

Dad was delighted to do as Ms Kindleson had asked because he loved her so much. And besides, no other grown-up, including those in his family showed him as much attention. She was like another mother to him. Smiling at her, he began the story. He began telling the giant's side of the story as if he was the giant.

"I was minding my own business, the business of counting gold, gold from my golden goose, and her golden eggs when suddenly I noticed, out of the corner of my eye a shadow of a small human figure scurrying about my abode. I turned to confront him, but he slithered away like a snake in the grass. I looked everywhere for him. I wanted to welcome him properly, but he was nowhere to be found. I became sad. The giant sobbed, 'I hardly ever have visitors. I'm so lonely-so alone in the world.'

It was getting late. Depression had set as the moon stood still in the mostly blackened sky. Pondering on the events of the day, the giant grew sadder and cried himself to sleep. Sleeping late into the morning was unusual for a giant. Not racing to the kitchen to fix breakfast was even more unusual. In fact, the giant only got up to see if the little human would come back. He had hoped that they would become good friends. Well, the little sneaky creature did not appear until darkness covered the sky and the moon took its place in the midst of sparkling lights and a few misplaced clouds hovering, finally floated past. The giant recalled what took place; almost bursting into tears.

'That night I awoke to a crash! It startled me and I was frightened. I'm afraid of monsters. My coat, hanging next to my closet looked like a big black blob with bulging eyes. I put my head underneath the covers, hoping that the invader of my castle would leave as quickly as he came. I then heard little feet tapping across my beautifully tiled living room floor. It was a familiar sound. I slowly removed the covers as I slipped quietly out of bed. I put on my slippers because the floor was cold. Aha! There he goes again that little thief! He was running towards the door with something in his arms. The door was open. I always leave it open. No one has ever come into my home unannounced before. The crime rate is nonexistent. That's why I could not believe it! That boy is stealing my goose! Now, I am angry! I would have shared my fortune with him if he would have only asked me to. I would have only asked for friendship in return. Now, I must punish this invader of my world and home! The giant was huffing and puffing while gaining on the invader. However, he was too out of shape. He thought to himself, 'boy he runs fast!' The young boy scampered to the bean stalk and climbed down it very fast! The giant thought to himself, 'I am too slow and clumsy. I may fall if I try to go too fast. He finally got to the bean stalk and began slowly climbing down when noticing that it was unsteady because someone was trying to cut it down. He climbed up to safety in time to yell down below, I'll never trust little humans again no matter how lonely it gets up here!"

Ending the story with incredible lucidity, dad waited for Ms Kindleson to respond. Ms Kindleson was stunned by the creativity she had just witnessed. *"What imagination,"* she exclaimed! And then she gave dad the biggest hug anyone had ever given him! *"What was that for?"* dad asked. Ms Kindleson replied, *"for being you, sweetie, for being the unique person you are, for being a thinker."* From that day forward he thought about how wonderful it would be if they forged a relationship, like the one he longed for with a mother figure. He could never have too many. This world needed more women willing to take on the job. Their bond would be fashioned into a memorable union made somewhere above the stars. He would cling to her for guidance and approval. He knew that she saw something in him, a talent and maybe an unexplored gift for seeing things in a way that few did or cared to mention. He would never forget that moment, that day either. The story he told Ms Kindleson stayed with him for years to come.

As if embarrassed, staring at the wall in the psychiatrist's office, he mumbled, *"it was a lesson for the unwise, the trusting and the innocent giants of the world."* The therapist asked him to expound on the statement just made. He said, *"at some point we all experience figurative giantism within and without. The anomaly of swollen hearts, filled with quests to give sometimes draws swindlers and thieves of good, who take and never give."*

Dad explained in more detail how later he realised that often people would come and go in his life: some for obvious reasons and others for not so obvious reasons. Learning where important characters like his mother, father, sisters, brothers, close relatives, and others fit would prove to be part of a puzzle that would take him a lifetime to match pieces and assemble the whole and make sense of life's experiences. People like Ms Kindleson and other spiritual mothers that he would later connect with proved to be much easier pieces of his life-puzzle to assemble or assimilate into what made him who he was and would become. They considered who or what he was as he absorbed who they were. Their significant roles played in his life's drama and their souls and beings, or existence meshed naturally with his as part of some bigger supernatural occurrence. They knew him and he them.

After dad's mother died, his sister who always looked after him and often held him tightly close to her whenever he wasn't with Aunt Ruthie, Uncle Charlie and their children, loved him deeply. Whenever they sat together in the evening with the rest of their brothers and sister on the flowery pink, red, and blue couch, and on the floor in the cramped living room space, her baby brother received the most attention from her. They talked about a lot of things because he loved hearing her thoughts on various subjects. The second saddest day of his life was when she went off to college. She'd hope to get the education that mum wanted her girls to have. It was hard for her to leave him behind. But how could she fulfill both promises made simultaneously to their mom, that had already required much sacrifice of her own youthful desires. She was supposed to take care of him in the same way mum would have done, while at the same time attend a good post-secondary school. She also kept in her mind the enormous responsibility that weighed her young heart of making sure Grandpop would be OK too, while trying to figure out who she was. That wasn't all that burdened her. Like many normal young adult female humans, she was in love with a young adult male human who made request of her too. Overwhelmed, but she wouldn't be overcome by the pressures that others of her generation and peer group succumbed too. So many people needed her, and she had her own needs too, with so much strength, she could handle it all and some if she needed too. It was through her that JT learned how to escape from that little town that spun a web, a trap, and took so many unsuspecting lives while still in their youth.

With his sister's departure, his mother's demise, and his dad working sixteen-hour shifts at the local factory and a part-time job selling vegetables and fruit, my dad experienced what he believed was one analogous axiom after the next to the beanstalk story. Dad was a little person with giant-size dreams and aspirations. As he gained self-esteem, knowledge, and realization of talents he possessed and predicted possibilities while not being naïve to his own limitations within this temporal world; from time-to-time small-minded people with ill-intentions would slip into his life, taking what they wanted from him whenever it pleased them to do so, leaving him with anger and disappointment. Dad found himself chasing thief after thief to the middle of the stalk. Each time he just yelled angrily down the beanstalk a warning that he'll not trust any human again.

Like the comedian Rodney Dangerfield would say, *"No respect."* Who could blame them, dad thought? *"I was a wimp, a pushover, a door mat, a busta and all other clichés descriptive of people, who were weak, and all talk and no action."* Deep down, he knew that would later change. He wouldn't always be a little boy, and everyone would see that Ms Kindleson was right. He was unique. He did things in a unique way, a way that's most of the time the right way. Once realizing that he had strayed or detoured from the right path, he humbly would go into the right direction. One of the things that his friends admired about dad was that he put forth the effort to show them how to do as well as one can when they could turn towards the right path. He confessed often that he wasn't as perfect as he would like to be, but that didn't stop him from trying. As a grown-up he became a real leader of his household as well as the community he belonged to. Mentor-leaders have many enormous responsibilities, and dad did not take his responsibilities lightly.

He found that real leaders, as found in popular studies, lead and rarely follow others without the wisdom and insight to do so first. That insight and wisdom comes from someone bigger than themselves. Speaking from a spiritual point of view, he had realised over the years that God is more than just self-righteous attitude. He is beyond understanding of religion. He is the God of survivors and those who graduated to thriving. The little boy with big dreams had survived and one day he would answer the call to be more and to receive the healing he deserved. Knowers matured at each developmental stage, or they were caged and controlled in hospitals. Something within dad, an augur moment perhaps, signaled a foretelling of things to come. A flame was lit within that little boy that would not be put out in his lifetime. As he grew up, a gentle giant in difficult times, he wrestled with becoming, yet he became the Knower beyond what anyone could imagine. Along his life's path, he gravitated towards certain positive personality types and kindred spirits.

Few adults had the positive affect on him that Aunt Ruthie and Ms Kindleson had. Dad knew her to be a wonderful mother to her own children, like Aunt Ruthie. She seemed to be like the perfect mothers he saw later on in the 1980's Kool-Aid commercials, he loved her warm wide-mouth smile. Those mothers were happy and strong and didn't seem to be the type to leave their babies alone, not even to make Kool-aid. Children in dad's neighbourhood needed that kind of mother. Single dads advertised and interviewed women, hoping one of them would be the one.

My Grandpop was one of those dads who was in the market for a qualified mothering companion type. It had been two years since his Etta passed on to her eternal resting place. Grandpop tried his best to provide much of what his children needed, but a mother's nurturing and mannerisms could not be mimicked nor be simulated. Dad's sisters came to this realization early on. When they took on the challenge made by my grandmother in those last dying moments; emotions were running high. I think they would have done and agreed to anything my grandmother would have asked in those last moments. My poor aunts and Grandpop were tasked with a mission that proved much more difficult to complete with the perfection and skill that my dying grandmother was much more suited for.

Dad jokes sometimes about the day his father announced that he was getting married to dad's stepmother to-be. To dad, he thought that she would be little more than a glorified live-in babysitter. He suspected that Grandpop did not marry for the love dad heard famous songsters croon about. Dad started suspecting the day Grandpop remarked, *"You boys need a mother."* Grandpop wasn't moved by dad's assurance that everyone was fine with the current arrangements. The little house had been filled with signs of a habitation of the grief-strickened since Grandma Etta had died. Each of dad's siblings seemed to be accustomed to being motherless. Shaped in motherless existence, why shouldn't anyone want to sustain the way of life that became vaguely familiar, the new norm. Dad referred to their new way of life as the abysmal culture of individual loneliness and void. The boys in his family were younger than their sisters who both were no longer living at home, each offspring saw the world differently than the others, but agreed that they objected to the notion and observation that they needed more than what Grandpop was willing or could honestly give to his children.

Nevertheless, without heeding their objections, Grandpop succeeded in finding someone to fill the vacancy of motherhood. Dad referred to her as the nanny at first. He and his siblings officially had a new mother whose main responsibility was to teach them proper etiquette and English and keep them out of trouble. With that being the case, my Grandpop's house was once again a two-parent household. Whenever Grand Pop's new bride walked into a room, it was a grand entrance.

Well nourished, first sight of her was seen from the back, which was hard not to notice. Dad remembered seeing what seemed like two hams in a bag, moving side to side, while trying not to burst from the seams of its wrappings. She was walking up the steps and onto the unfinished screened porch towards the entrance of the modest Jim Walter Home. Inside, everything was plain and cheap. Most of the furniture was found on the side of streets, in front of houses that had been condemned to demolition because their bones were not the good ones in which renovation would be successful or those on which new construction hung. The fresh smell of young timber was long gone too from most homes on dad's street. Although the strong candidate that had been named his new mother didn't seem to mind as far as anyone could tell, she was seen writing a note to herself in a little writing tablet.

Placing her writing material and tools in her bag, then looking around once again through dark, round sunglasses, soon after her first words spoken to dad and his big brothers that were two, four, six, and eight years older than him was *"you can call me mother."* It had begun, the nerve of this woman; she was already trying to tell them what to do! Mother of whom, is what dad wanted to ask, but he knew Grandpop would do to him what was considered child abuse in society today, and so he quietly fumed within and thought, *"My mother died and was reincarnated, and I'll meet her again someday,"* dad thought to himself; *she'll have a new name, but she'll be just as beautiful, considerate, and warm as before she left the first time."* It was dad's great imagination that kept Etta with him, her memory alive and he wasn't about to let a mommy substitute come in and completely erase her from his heart and mind. Even if his stepmother offered him a whopping five dollars so that he may warm to her, it wouldn't be enough. No amount would be enough to dissuade him of loyalty to Etta. If he could have sent a public service message to any stepparents to-be, he would have warned them that bribery was not the answer, and that money couldn't buy you love. Sooner or later a person must be themselves and hopefully have a winning personality. To win a child over you must have the *"it-factor,"* genuine ability to love unconditionally. It is that little something that comes naturally with being a credible good human being. You must be natural at parenting, putting yourself last and putting children first. Sometimes biological parents and stepparents discover in the eleventh hour, at the first temper tantrum, that they are terrible at loving others deeply, especially children.

    At six, dad knew the difference between unnatural parenting and natural parenting. In his small town, there were natural parents and then there were those who played the role of one. It is sort of like the actor or actress who over acts a part. They are sincere about the part, but the part is just not for them, or they needed more talent and enormous private tutoring.

Dad's stepmother really wanted to be a good mother to my dad and maybe if she had a world class acting coach, she would have achieved parenting excellence.

Dad had remarked once, remembering, that *"she received high marks in cooking, cleaning, mentoring, tutoring, and bossiness. Yet, her naturalness to motherly affection and ability to know when to become the mother bear was lacking somewhat. Although we evaluated and graded on the curve, she still failed in several ways, no matter how hard she tried."* As far as Grandpop, the obvious head of the household was concerned, like a star athlete, she received a passing grade in all subjects, whether she deserved it or not.

Out of the other members of the household, Grandpop's youngest child graded her least hard. The other grades from the other graders were typical and signified what was apparent. Grandpop thought he was doing the most sensible thing he could do for his boys, but things did not look good for her. There were no whistles and applauses from the audience. The only thing she had going in her favor was the youngest boy's smile and nod of approval because he felt sorry for her. Youngest children hold a special power within the single-parent household. And for dad's efforts he received an unspoken, but an enthusiastic facial expression that signaled a bond, acceptance and agreement between he and she, contingent upon her cementing a loving relationship from the power-that-mattered in the household, the patriarch, Grandpop. Dad's brother, seven years older than him, mumbled under his breath to another brother sighing deeply, *"do not collect $200.00 and pass go."* The other brother nodded his head and with eyes glaring he mumbled under his breath, *"You dang right big bro."* Grandpop caught the two brothers communicating amongst themselves; he gave them a frightening look because he thought it was rude to whisper during important moments like this one. They quickly thought to make peace with their father and stepped towards the lady they were forced to call *"motha."* One of the brothers' first thought was to politely shake her hand, but he knew that would not due. He knew he had to pretend that he felt an instant kinship, a natural something. With his body language he lied. He lied to her, Grandpop, and all who witnessed the misguided notion, God and the entire group of people who made up the world around him. There was nothing seemingly natural about what was happening there between him, her, and the rest of the family. He felt he and his siblings were on the auction block. They were being looked over like animals. They met their new master's approval. Another's property, they had to accept their fate like the powerless victims they had become, their rights to choose a replacement mum trampled on.

Often, dad looks back on that day. Saddened that the transition time of his mother's passing into the afterlife and the entering of his stepmother through the backdoor of temporal life, contributed to the genesis of his gradual mental fragility and him becoming guarded against an invisible enemy, as well as losing the wife of his youth my mom, the love of his life.

At night before getting into bed, in the morning before rising from bed, and before any appointment and meeting, dad's prayer became, *"Lord, organise my thoughts, order my steps."* If the mantra had been adhered to religiously and consistently each day of his life, maybe dad would have shown leadership, been the first to show genuine, full acceptance, and more transparent compassion towards his stepmother, and less cowardice fear towards the invisible enemy and fierce protection of my mom, my sister and me, to keep our family together. Grandpop would have been proud of him.

It was the part of my dad, JT, that Grandpop appreciated, he possessed Grandma Etta's genes. Her blood within him was a gift and curse, but with balance and the strength from Grandpop's genes, their son would suffer only mild symptoms of mental illness and would be protected from the complete madness other Knowers succumbed too. By the same token, Etta's blood could not protect JT from the beast his dad's, my Grandpop's cancerous blood cells planted genetically within him and had originated within Grandpop's ancestors long ago.

Chapter Four

The battle with the beast would overshadow all previous battles for both of them, Grandpop and dad. Like military battles, the emotional, mental, and physical violent struggles together were a holistic perfect storm that could destroy a few or many lives. During both their battles with the beast that would lay claim to both their lives eventually, each experienced a life flashing before their eyes event.

With his eyes, my Grandpop spoke volumes to his children. JT's brother, two years older than dad, had until that moment distanced himself from everyone in the room, sat in a corner waiting until grandpop's eye summoned him to centre stage. The spotlight was now on him, and it shined brightly. He was sweating and it was noticeable. Poor guy, he was going to suffer for his tough, stubborn attitude. JT felt so sorry for him and at the same time he felt such admiration for his big brother who seemed much braver than him. However, dad wasn't sure that his hero would live long enough to receive the accolades and medals due to him for a battle that could not be won by mortal men; to say the least, little boys. Not surprisingly, before long dad heard a thump! In his words, remembering, *"my brother flew forward and off balance and almost landed in the nanny's lap, but then quickly stepped back and waited, careful not to look directly into her eyes and be turned to stone. She too waited, her face darkened, as did her mood. In silence, she just seemed to be waiting for something. Not getting what she expected, she stepped towards my brother and gave him a church hug; butt in the air while arms extended without touching from the waist down, she collapsed her large frame around his smaller one."* For some minutes dad only caught a glimpse of the tips of his big brother's fingernails; they showed signs of life as they wiggled and changed to a pink colour. Dad gasped in amazement at his brother's herculean will and effort to survive. Squirming and finally able to free himself, he gave her a funny look and sprinted back towards the other siblings. Escaping towards their direction he knew he would find refuge, but before crossing into that safe zone, he was knocked off balance with another one of my grandfather's heavy hands. Slowly rising to his feet and then waiting for permission to leave, he made the disapproving faces of a boy who was not pleased with his lot in life, the expected way things were in the family chosen for him.

He stood as still as a statue before his tormentors, until finally his father felt he had suffered enough. Embarrassed and nearly defeated, JT's big brother returned to his corner, far away from enemy lines. With his eyes, his little brother congratulated him on his efforts. He had stood up and faced danger with little success, but he showed no cowardice. Dad was proud of him while recollecting that his big brother had almost gave up the ghost for a lost cause. That brother was a rebel if ever dad had seen one, but not one without a cause, noble or not.

As JT watched the scene of his father, and his new wife and his big brothers' interaction, he realised that day was more of a bizarre twist of fate than anything else. Grandpop had married on his children's biological mom's birthday. Etta's baby boy had felt himself getting lightheaded and then, thump!

His brother that was seven years older than him, told dad later that this was the first time that he had seen their father look afraid. No tears yet, but he had a look of fear and anyone that knew him knew that this was not the norm. The lady that said, *"call me motha"* didn't know how to react either and panicked, so his other brother ended up calling 911, being that he was the only one that seemed to not be in shock and well composed. At family reunions, the brother often reminded JT that he owed him his life, he had stopped breathing and the 911 operator guided the brother through CPR, especially the uncomfortable touching lip to corner of mouth, sealing the passageway to the lungs. Rarely known for his altruistic activity, sharing his own breaths with his little brother was a big deal. Grandpop was thankful, to say the least, but he didn't seem himself.

It was as if Etta's day of birth was a strain on Grandpop's mental health and was affecting him too. The calendar would no longer mark it ever happening. Another celebrated event would take its place. The thought of dad's mother being replaced by the nanny was too much for him and for Etta's baby boy to handle, but it was never to be spoken of, but that past event along with many others dominated Grandpop's and JT's psyche and clouded the narrative they shared during their years together in the small town.

JT, born during what seemed challenging times for his family, an experience that would bound Grandpop and Etta closer together as a couple. It was predicted that most of JT's life would be plagued with sickness, noticed mostly during emotional, mental, and physically taxing activities. Not wanting his son to miss out on the gifts that life would offer despite what seemed disabilities, Grandpop pushed his youngest child to aim as high as possible, to surpass his own seemingly lesser abilities. Secretly, Grandpop wrestled with darkness and doubt. His mind was often filled with negative thoughts. He had not accepted and could not handle the possibility, nor did he want to ever witness his youngest son, JT's inevitable ill fate, he felt he had to remain hopeful about his son's future. The nightly attack of insomnia and falling asleep during the day when he should have been working nearly cost him his job. When he did sleep a recurring nightmare would affect his quality of sleep. Grandpop wasn't sure which was worse, insomnia or sleeping poorly. Sometimes Etta would appear in his dreams, and he would wake soon afterward and see the same 3:15 a.m. time appear on the little clock on the dresser across from the double bed on which he lay staring up at the ceiling. Like clockwork, his breathing caught his eyes, and he began counting breaths as his chest moved in a rhythm with the ticking. Soon, he was fast asleep and running as fast as he could from a beast that was set on devouring him whole, one piece at a time. This happened night after night and one last time the night before JT's high school graduation. On the night of his son's graduation, the insomnia returned and then something peculiar happened.

It was late and Grandpop was tossing and turning, not able to fall asleep, Etta's voice was heard coming from the dimly lit room during a rather unusual starry night. Gathering his strength wasn't as hard at that moment. It had been difficult that week to will himself beyond the small living quarters he shared with his second wife, but the voice seemed to give him strength and his feet seemed to slide forward and across like the crowned King of Pop, Michael Jackson on a stage during one of his concerts. Not long after, he stood in the narrow hallway peering into the small hole of the unleveled wall and into the family room. Through the cracked opening, he couldn't believe what his eyes revealed. It was like watching an old silent film, but there wasn't a projector and reels. Excitedly, removing his eye from its place in the wall, walking stealthily to the doorway of the family room, he craned his neck and half salt and peppered balding scalp in the shape of a shepherd's staff, bracing the frame of the door, closest to the jamb, his breath fogging the top hinge. The Looking Glass heirloom flickered black and white pictures in noiseless motion, partly visible next to the decorative wooden clock Aunt Ruthie had bought at a yard sale, but thought it looked better at her big brother's house. Surprised to witness the paranormal activity, attracted to the floor, Grandpop's bending knees connected and slid across the cheap linoleum, tearing his pajamas, the Walmart Christmas present he received two years before. The future was the past and the data shown on the Looking Glass screen streamed backwards. His youngest son's life passed before him in almost a flash.

 JT grew stronger and before long he was playing with his friends and doing things just as well as other little boys. Although everything seemed OK with him, his father didn't take any chances. He made him rest often and when he came home from work, he would first check on him before doing anything else. Sometimes he would call from a pay phone during lunch or before leaving work and ask him how his day was going. He would often say to him, *"Read, boy,"* before placing the phone's handset, transmitter and receiver snuggly on the cradle hook. JT admitted often that he didn't like reading as much as he liked playing basketball or football at first, but it was the one thing that didn't tire him out so fast. Soon, he began to love reading more than any other activity. Using his imagination, he could see the actions that were taking place in those books. He saw men fighting wars and kings making courageous men into knights of shining armor and their ladies wishing them well before going off to battle. He saw faraway lands and strange people dressed in strange garments and animals that had hard-to-pronounce names. He learned that his small corner of the world was vastly different in cultural norms from seventy-five per cent of the international community. At eighteen years of age, he knew he wanted to see it in person and confirm what was written in the textbooks and historical novellas. The day came and his father didn't wait for him to start the conversation about his dreams and plans to seek what he needed to see and experience in the other three fourths of the world. *"Go boy, it's ok,"* were some of his exact words.

Tears streamed down the face of Grandpop, the weathered middle-aged man who longed to discover a fountain of youth and health and thrive in the second chapter of a new life on earth before entering the eternal one in heaven. His work for many years had been with his hands and outdoors from sunup to sundown. The hand in life he had been dealt was hard, but he was intentional about never letting anyone hear him complain about it, especially his children. If they had more than he had growing up in a hard world, he was grateful and satisfied. Often, he thought, *"time waits on no man."* Yesterday a blur, today would be gone in a blink, and tomorrow will be the present burrowing for only a moment in its temporary home and then back to the past. The only love he knew how to give wasn't wrapped in kisses and hugs, smiles, and nods of approval. For him, a demonstration of love wasn't displayed in those ways. Doing love was more his style. Sheltering, feeding, clothing, and protecting was the way he did love. In his mind, the legacy passed to his children would be the things that mattered, and they would pass them to their children. Making things better for the next generation would be their mission, mandate, and badge of honour. He drew strength from his faith and feeling that his sacrifice would not be in vain. Those before him had known painful poverty. He only needed to taste it as a boy before swearing that he would do everything in his power to escape its effects on the human consciousness. He would make sure his future wife and children would not know the ugliness of poverty. As members of the working poor, they would know a better life. Struggle had no mercy on this much worn-out worker who barely escaped the clutches of generational poverty. It seemed the harder he worked the poorer Etta, and the children became. Only experiencing more grief after Etta's passing, winning didn't seem possible while here on earth. Poor guy, what would become of him? He wasn't comforted anymore by the fact that he had weathered similar storms or had known nothing, but poverty growing up and being poor was supposed to be better, new tracks along new stations of the hard life's journey.

Grandpop was the eldest of my great grandmother's nine children. He became father figure and provider for them at the tender and impressionable age of fifteen, July 18, 1942. Not old enough to go to war, but old enough to be a casualty of the war waged by poverty, bigotry, and inequality. The land settled by his mother and grandmother, and the children in tow wasn't sold or rented legally to them. Squatters, they lived in a two-room shack next to what was coupled as a chicken coop and food pantry. It wasn't unusual for them to scoop the chicken poop out of the flour so that they could use the flour to make bread and gravy for dinner. My great grandmother had stored the flour in a 132oz tin can which had a few tiny holes in the rusty lid. When I first heard the story, I frowned and held my stomach as if appalled or grossed out from the picture formed in my mind of my Grandpop scooping out small clumps of chicken feces.

It was clear to all of his children that Grandpop's younger life had been hard and it affected him in every way possible especially his effort to form healthy relationships with family and friends. My dad, uncles, and aunts, seeing their father from the perspective of poverty informed, grew compassionate in their understanding of him years later when they reflected deeply about how he became the person they had only known in their current short lifetime. Born only a few years after the first war during a depression that devastated whole groups of people, they could have only imagined the despair he and others of his generation may have experienced. Aunt Ruthie, born second to the last child, knew some of the pain of being brought up in slightly impoverished conditions. Her hero, big brother, and father figure had bore the weight of bread winner responsibilities; his emotional, mental, spiritual, and physical strength seemingly superhuman and she could hardly tell if any of what he had inherited were a nuisance or challenge in anyway. Working long tiring weeks earned him admiration among those he loved and wages that kept the family a little more than afloat for many years.

The stories that she told birth tears of both sorrow and joy. Her brother seemed invincible and never on the brink of brokenness, even as the chasm between him, a member of the have nots, and those who enjoyed having more than enough widened. His facial expression and actions always revealed a penchant to remain determined to embrace what became his burden to carry alone. A man of few words, but known for the meaningful and thoughtful verbal contributions to conversations, his words were not minced nor wasted. Those closest to him sometimes misunderstood him. Secretly, he longed to show the transparency that was unknown to his younger siblings and his own children. In the end, only his beautiful Etta would know him well. To the grave, she would take his secrets, his ambitions. Their youngest son, a Knower, would stumble upon past truths that the father owned, and the mother valued.

Buried beneath what seemed obvious and on the surface was something much more than many who met him guessed to be true. Looking beyond the bulging muscles, the fierce look in his eyes when he focused on the things that mattered to him could prove difficult. Etta would say that his heart muscle was softer than his facial appearance and other visible hardness. Her ability to read his emotional state was remarkable and it made her his rock and their relationship brought balance to the household. Etta and Aunt Ruthie were his allies. Together, they protected him and provided him with wise counsel as well. Losing Etta to the great beyond left him feeling in pieces. Wholeness remained out of his grasp for the foreseeable future, even after he married a second time. Aunt Ruthie was the only one who seemed to understand his rationale for remarrying, even if the timing seemed a little questionable. Etta and her big brother had been there during the darkest moments while her Charlie was away and said to be missing from the Army in Vietnam. Now, Etta was missing in all their lives and darkness had once again enveloped their family.

It was a scary monster like the one hidden in the closets of children's bedrooms and in the cold sterile spaces of mental hospitals, quietly in the night it appeared during lights out. Like a frail child and mental patient, Grandpop faced his fear of the unknown without little hope of overcoming the enemy Aunt Ruthie and Etta fiercely protected him from. His second wife was unaware of the affliction and would remain so until the end of her life. Like certain types of anemia, Grandpop's affliction was an inherited disease. It was a disorder that was seen through signs such as emotional crushing of others, especially children, lovers, friends, pets, admirers, and anyone who dared cross the paths of those with the disease, whether in relationships or as strangers. Family members struggled with his or her own shackles that confined them to limited proper socialization, but few of them understood why and how to escape the cycle of misery to self and others. Freedom would only come through renewed ways of thinking. JT realised this when he started looking at his own pattern. Changes in his own behavior was needed, especially after hearing Aunt Ruthie tell stories about his father as a teenager. A lot of it was sad, some funny, but weird. Those that knew Grandpop best could help JT know him and help him not repeat the same mistakes his dad made. Maybe that's why Grandpop always told him to read. He wanted him to learn a better way of being.

There were various subjects or topics to read and the more he read the more he changed his thinking and his behavior. Also, a hunger developed and grew within him to know more. He was the youngest and no matter how old or intelligent he grew with time and knowledge he was still viewed as the little brother and nothing he did or said was taken seriously. It wasn't long before he learned to play the game. It was one of pretend. Inside, he knew a lot more than he would say. Outside, his lips were sealed, he played the quiet game. His stepmother would always look at him curiously. Never saying a word about what she was thinking, but her eyes spoke volumes to him. His eyes answered her questions. Their conversation was held in an unusual way, but it was more useful than morse code. One year, for JT's birthday, she bought him a journal. She wrote inside the front cover, *"for your journey."* Somehow, she knew. JT longed to go away to where he felt he belonged. There was a place in the world for him. For years, he would search for that place. Restless, as a young man, he didn't dare to stop, to put down roots. In the first chapter of his life, he hardly saw his siblings, Aunt Ruthie and his cousins. Without the object he needed most, his searching was done with little guidance and purpose.

Aunt Ruthie had promised Etta she would keep an eye on him and his progress. She and Keila would be in his life as much as he would allow. He would need them more than he realised. Journaling on the journey would serve its purpose of holding his thoughts on pages. The madness was kept in check if he journaled.

However, the journal could not be a true companion. It only knew what he told it. Holding knowledge was different from holding conversations with a living being. There were some things that JT wanted to know that he didn't know and wouldn't know until he met with other living beings that knew those things that would keep the madness away always.

Uncle Charlie had taught him one way of keeping the madness away for a couple of hours. Fishing was the physical activity that quieted and slowed JT's active mind long enough to accept the peace that longed to fill him. For him, fishing was yoga. It was therapeutic during the longing for simpler times and stillness. Fishing brought not only physical nourishment through the catch, but fed the person emotionally too. Mentally, healing was welcomed.

Grandpop appreciated Uncle Charlie's attention to his youngest son, but he believed that JT needed more than leisurely activities to fill his day. Life was hard and he needed a hardened mind and heart. Intentionally becoming cerebral would prepare him for the hard things he would encounter when Grandpop would no longer be around. Grandpop had learned this personally to help him handle life's ups and downs, and hard choices through human developmental stages. Fearing that his youngest son would become prey to the predators who stalked the young and inexperienced, he hoped to protect Etta's baby boy from heartache and the harsher penalties of naiveness.

In his heart he longed to be a good father and not repeat the mistakes made with his other children. To his surprise, JT was willing to listen and he hung on every word that flung from his dad's mouth as they tossed the meanings of their word game back and forth in the space between them as easily as two would throw a ball in the air while standing on a grassy field. It was one of those rare bonding moments experienced between father and son. Nervously, Grandpop had taken Aunt Ruthie's advice about being open and honest about his own personal experiences along his own personal journey.

No journal of his own, the words from his heart, mind, and mouth would be written on JT's mental pages and absorbed into his Corazón. Grandpop spoke of the various knowledge gained from experiences that was the forbidden fruit that he longed to possess for more than just viewing, simply because he was warned of the effect it could have on his behavior and reputation. During JT's first chapter in life, he experienced the same struggles that his father tried to help him avoid. Grandpop knew that there was something that JT would eventually know, but was at the age for which it was better if he didn't, but what would happen was inevitable. Keeping him in the dark for much longer would prove futile. Now seemingly aging rapidly, Etta, his sounding board and better half gone into eternity, and just feeling that the time had come, Grandpop knew that it was better that JT heard from him the things that were good to experience and those that were not good to see, hear, taste, nor touch. Etta's dying wish was that the two would bond through words with deep lasting meaning and not just through outdoor activities, sports, and the usual things that cause fathers and sons to become close. Grandpop told JT to *"protect your senses boy. Practice being highly sensitive to the dangers in your path. Your mother could see them before anyone else. She saw the future in the past. Everything she heard was remembered too. Etta's favorite sayings that her mamma would repeat from time to time, was 'taste and see that the Lord is good. Touch the hem of his garment,' when you need his goodness to touch your soul. Our Creator wants his creation to experience certain things in this life that help us forget as much as we can about the evil and sin in this temporal world."*

Perhaps his dad held in his mind the account of the first earth humans recorded in the creation story, although his youngest son seemed more curious about the everyday practical science that helped make sense of nature and all living things, he was attentive to his father's wise counsel and listened intently to the serious meaning behind his words. When JT would hear his father say, "*son,*" he leaned forward wherever he was sitting. "*Son, they too wanted to know what they didn't need to know. As the story goes, they failed to push away curiosity and soon their desire to know opened their eyes to a world of hardship. Like many of us who are confronted by temptation much of our lives; these first humans found it hard to just say no. Like them, much of my life has been spent in slavery. I have been a slave to desire-the desire to know, be, and do. Like a magnet, I'm drawn to other people's lives. I want to know them and others who have relationships with them. After allowing myself to know them I end up being sucked further into their world. Their world is a soap opera. Before long I become one of the many characters in each scene. Not sure whether I am coming or going, I am just there. Existing for their pleasure I remain there. And I do what they desire that I do because deep down inside of myself is the desire to do what they desire I do. I want them and everyone in their world to accept me. Existing in the world for the sole purpose of housing soap opera characters isn't good for the soul and isn't one that will exist for very long. My role has become one of tortured instability. At midlife, I'm still learning the importance of stability and balance. If I could learn to only allow encouragement to begin the journey of healing and the quest for finding a continued middle ground. Maybe this will be possible once I'm afforded the courage to confront the demons of my past. See me JT Be careful to study my face and its changes. Hear me JT What am I saying and what am I not saying?"*

Without warning, Grandpop burst into laughter. Apologizing for digressing and babbling, he spoke more clearly without much riddle, instead he verbally summarised his memoir before abruptly walking away from his middle school tween.

Born the oldest to a single mum and an often-absent father, Grandpop was the product of an unstable home life and unhappy childhood. His mum was less educated than probably sixty per cent of the young women her age, but smart and quickly learned the ways of the world. Grandpop remembered her to be very loving, but worked hard and wasn't home much in his earlier years growing up. His grandmother took care of him and his younger siblings while his mum was away slaving as a house maid, and engaged in other hustles, to aid the family's survival. Some grandmothers are nice, and others are mean or fall somewhere in between. Grandpop experienced mostly in between or mean. Bipolar wasn't a word he heard in his early days on earth, but was used frequently once his youngest son, JT, was born. As a growing wordsmith, it was a term that he could use from his collection of words to finally sufficiently describe his grandmother. Her moodiness created anxiety for Grandpop and his siblings whenever they were around her, even when they were older.

Whenever they were able to, they would sneak off to a place they considered to be a refuge. A safe place was mostly what they desired more than anything else growing up. Grandpop often said that they lived through two Great Depressions, the one that clouded his grandma's thinking and the one that poor people didn't understand, but the rich couldn't stop talking about. He dreamt of becoming rich if not only to leave at least one of the depressions behind and never to experience it again and maybe even write a book about how he did it and sell it and become even richer. Great Grandmother didn't encourage daydreams, big dreams, or dreams of any kind. Only impressed by hard work and positive results, she frequently screamed, cussed, scowled, and rolled her eyes while reminding him that if he wasn't careful, he would be good for nothing like his sorry sperm donor. Grandpop hated the disrespectful colourful language and the reminder that his father was a failure and that there were signs of his inherited genetic material visibly present in him. The quest to prove her wrong began and the obsession to do so led to physical and mental signs of decay, as he juggled school assignments and penciled in the remaining times each day with employment opportunities. Eight-hour rest periods became as extinct as the T-Rex.

When he wasn't working odd jobs as a teen, Grandpop hung out with peers who had at six and seven years old seen their first pictures of naked people, some posing for the camera, others were doing other things with a partner. These were things that his virgin ears received gladly, and his brain kept a detailed record, and he didn't understand why, but another part of his body had received a message from the brain clearly and responded naturally to its transmission. His whole life, the images described by his peers would play back in his daydreams and at night as he went into a deep sleep. The first time he awoke to the embarrassment of the response of his body to the running away of his imagination into the strange place that he tried hard not to go into, he quickly dismissed it as bedwetting and hid the forensic evidence, not wanting to discuss nor debate its existence.

Later, he would say to himself that this forbidden knowledge offered to him in innocence caused him to lose his place in Eden. For most of his life, he felt guilt and shame and wanted to be rid of it. Finally, one day he talked to an old traveling preacher who told him how to make the awful thoughts go away. One part of the instructions given about confessing was easy, but the believing that it could happen and how it could happen was confusing to him. Yet, as he thought about the alternative of living with the stuff that contended for his attention and invaded his dreams day and night, in desperation he cried to the God that the old traveling preacher said would help him if he believed in that God and His power to heal the sick and save the lost.

Grandpop hadn't thought that he was sick and lost, but he guessed some of it was true because most of the time he didn't feel well in the head and stomach. The lost part, he had to think more about, although he felt he had lost something, he felt too that something else was vying to take its place within him. A struggle between light and darkness manifested in intense reactions and extreme responses for the rest of his days with living friends and relatives who often remarked that he deserved grace and compassion because a hard life path had been carved out for him. The victory experienced through the increased presence of light in his remaining years was felt to be of epic proportions.

Etta had been his rock, each day, knowing her understanding, forgiveness, and patience was available, he felt renewed and hopeful. Like Grandpop, she was the oldest in her family and understood the weight of being responsible for younger siblings and carried it with pride, knowing that she was able to help her family survive in the worst of times and possibly thrive in the best of times. She was the female version of Grandpop. Their parents approved of their seemingly instant connection and glad that they were right for each other.

They were more right than they realised for more reasons than one. Unbeknownst to Grandpop, Etta knew him before he knew her. It would be many years later that she would reveal her secret to him. Once it was revealed, he said to her, *"I always felt that it was something mysterious about you that attracted me to you, but I never understood the what and why of it until now."* She only smiled sheepishly. She loved him deeply before meeting him. He needed her before meeting her and loved her at first sight.

He, the strong silent type, and she was bashful with kind beautiful eyes. The dimples that formed the valley of each of Etta's cheeks brought delight to Grandpop whenever he saw her. Without warning he would softly kiss each one. Each day together was special to both of them, but Grandpop didn't know why he felt that way. He wondered if Etta felt the strangeness of time slipping away from them each second too. He detested being away from her and could hardly wait to be back by her side, loving her with every ounce of his being. Etta understood him better than anyone else. She knew his thoughts and finished his sentences. Etta knew his dreams and wanted them all to come true, but knew that they would all only come true through his children. Through them, Grandpop would live and so would his dreams. Unlike his grandmother, Etta encouraged him to slow down and let the dreams wash over his being, cooling him in the heat of uncomfortable moments. Only one of his children would inherit that part of him and would struggle in a similar way to him, but through that son's pain and suffering the writer in the son would be wielded. His brothers would never experience his struggle, but they would still harness their tools and skills that would bring them success and so would their sisters.

    The girls were older, nurturing, and very caring too. Above all, they had brilliant, creative minds. The oldest one became a lawyer. The way she saw the world gave her an edge against any opponent in her profession. Gifted, she ripped through the opposing arguments like a human shredder. A reputation widely known, no litigator dared face her without a plan to win and a team worthy of her time. The fire in her eyes and sharp tongue came from Grandpop. The smoothness, ingenious wordsmithing, critical thinking part of her was inherited through Etta's DNA.

The youngest girl was a combination of gentle, a free-spirit, well-read, but above all else a prolific problem solver, no matter how many she faced. For much of her life from pre-school forward, she was known for being the peace maker in the family and no one was surprised when she graduated from the university with two degrees, one in sociology with a minor in anthropology and the other in world history, her eyes and mind set on becoming a future diplomat and play her part on the world stage. For a brief period of time, she entered the world of politics. First, she worked in the mayor's office of a nearby city with a population of five-thousand citizens. After four years of hard work and doing what she remarked as, watching from the sidelines, she felt she was being called to enter the City Council race. She could hear Etta's voice, *"the race is not given to the swift nor the battle to the strong, but to the one that endures to the end."* Her opponents were patient, older, skillful, ruthless, more experienced, and willing to put in the time while out working the other candidates smartly. Making up for what she lacked and to be first across the finish line, a gifted campaign manager was needed. Finding the right person would usually take more time than she had or was willing to give, but to her amazement the perfect person for the job had always believed that they were supposed to be partners in a couple of different scenarios. As she was thinking of him, the phone rang. It was as if they picked up where they left off in college, he a political science graduate and she the do gooder that would change the world. Together, they were a natural fit personally and professionally. Their college friends were not surprised to get an invitation to their wedding and to learn of their success in the field of politics and in the arena of love.

    Grandpop and Etta's boys had some success of their own too. Their three oldest sons went into business together as owners of an automobile dealership that had vehicle rental, mechanic, paint and wash details, and a business department. Overseeing over two-hundred employees with responsibilities that overlapped in other work areas, they hired brilliant supervisors to manage those areas and the heavy lifting that came with making everything go as smoothly as possible. Each of them was a gifted leader in his own way. Neither of them disappointed Grandpop and Etta in their work and lifestyle.

Etta knew that what they had accomplished would all come to pass and would ensure her grandchildren a hopeful future. It was all seen in the Looking Glass. Although she would never physically be a part of her children's later lives and experience their success and their challenges, she could know about it before it became a reality. This knowledge brought her both joy and sadness. Grandpop saw a few years of the reality that Etta would miss. It was a joy for him to see each of his children graduate from high school and continue their education post secondary. As he sat through the last graduation, he wept softly, thinking of Etta and the things that she told him would happen. His dream to graduate high school, college, and to own a business would not happen to him, but would happen to his children. Later that night after finally laying his head down, Grandpop dreamt again, but it would be the last time and it would be about his youngest son.

JT stood in front of a road that took the shape of a wishbone and then it became two roads. He could see for miles down both roads. Down one was a beautiful landscape on either side, but down the other was a thick growth of brush and weird-looking plants which marked where the road was, but covered the edges of its smooth surface. Suddenly, he heard a whisper. *"Choose."*

Chapter Five

He looked all around, but saw no one. He heard the voice say again, *"Choose. Youthful strength will take you far and wisdom will be your guide through life's rollercoaster journey."* Then he heard his name being called by what seemed like one voice, *"JT, JT it's time to go."* Turning his eyes towards the place the voice came, he saw Aunt Ruthie and Uncle Charlie standing near the road with the covered edges. *"Get going boy. There's no time to lose, but much to gain."* Aunt Ruthie quickly handed him a covered basket. An aroma delighted his nose. The bacon, biscuits, grits, eggs, and pancakes were still warm. He turned around to say thanks, but Aunt Ruthie and Uncle Charlie had slipped away. Only the sound of one voice remained behind. *"JT, we love you too and you're welcome. Eat now, leave the basket and then go."* Smiling ear to ear, he did as the voice said. It was enough to satisfy, but not enough to overfill. Aunt Ruthie and Uncle Charlie knew him way too well. With his energy level increased and his mind much clearer than before, the next thing to do was to begin the journey. Going the way of knowers would be interesting. He and Keila were the last in their family to go the way. Behind them would be their small town, family, friends, and the envious.

Preparing to walk the road with the covered edges, adjusting on his shoulder the old green military duffle bag Uncle Charlie had given him a few days earlier, packed, and ready for the adventure ahead, JT remembered reading as a class assignment a book on immigration entitled Fork in the Road. It was one of the most interesting readings he had experienced in high school. Each chapter was cerebral and focused on what it was like being a citizen of a nation, its culture, society, and politics. Often after each chapter he paused to reflect. In his small town he had not seen very many people who were born in another country. The ones he had met didn't speak English very well and were from a smaller country to the south. Uncle Charlie had said one time that some of them worked at the sawmill seasonally and each year left their homes behind and embarked on a journey up and over mountains, down into valleys, trekking often through treacherous thick underbrush to get to the foreign small town that would help feed their families and free themselves of the poverty that had bound their loved ones for generations. Uncle Charlie had remarked that there were always others who are worse off, they suffer at the bottom of the socioeconomic ladder. If they're lucky they climb up one or two rungs to a better place in life than the one below them.

Reading was one of the ways JT escaped his meager existence in a place he supposed should be called home, but never really felt that way for him, nor Keila, Aunt Ruthie, and Etta. Though neither of them discussed it ever, each of them always imagined leaving the small-town lifers behind and traveling and meeting new people and seeing strange new lands and experiencing someone else's customs, culture, in a foreign country.

Etta, in her youth never ventured out after falling in love with Grandpop and not long ladened with a mother's responsibility had missed her opportunity to go were the knowing called her to. Secretly, she knew her second chance would come through her baby boy. She would live her life to the fullest through him.

Carrying Etta in his heart, JT was led to a place along the road with covered edges where his throat seemed to need clearing and his lungs trying to fill up with fresh air almost collapsed from filling with pollution. Others were there too, where the road seemed to end. They too were there thinking about which way to go, while trying not to suffocate on an invisible foul substance. A thick gaseous foulness that clouded the environment strangled everyone that entered its territory. People, far too numerous to count, of all ages, colours, cultures, and social standing were there, trying to find their way to the one road that seemed to lead to nowhere. Some were members of the social elite while others fell in with the untouchables. Many fell somewhere in between the two groups. The commonality among all of them was the confusion and rapid depletion of hope that each person felt. They all searched for something that required more than excellent credit and collateral or the trading of currency and other valuables. Finding it would be a little more than a miracle. Its whereabout was the X on the treasure map that no one in the gathering knew how nor where to search for. A third of the group began fretting and making a commotion and then dispersed to the east and west, while another third turned to go back towards the direction they came from. The remaining third looked quietly towards the road's end that seemed to slowly extend in length and width. As if in a trance JT, no longer experiencing the choking sensation, moved around to the front of the crowd that stayed the course before them. Once in what seemed the designated area and position, he stepped forward and felt a breeze on his right cheek and a sweet fragrance in both nostrils.

The fog in his mind cleared simultaneously with the air around him and those standing near him were no longer strangers, but seemed familiar to him. Thinking and seeing clearly was a gift to the fellow travelers too, whose chatter no longer sounded confusing, but were joyful sounds of elation and laughter.

JT was not surprised to find emigrants and immigrants alike at the end of the road, coming and going; each salivating at the grass on the other side of state and national boundary; forgetting that everything always looks better in an exotic land. In fact, JT would have found it more surprising if he had not found any people coming and going at all. The promise of riches and glory has a way of luring dreamers of every nationality there and once hooked, they're reeled quickly into a society that cares only that they are a good catch.

There were people from little known places in the international community who came to find their way in a new and strange land. Each of their experiences was like the stories told in the Fork in the Road. Hopeful with a bit of desperation, it was then in the current present that families of various sizes launched expeditions that were either successful or disastrous. JT grew concerned about the souls around him. He wanted to help steer them to not just greener pastures, but safer ones too. But how could he? He was young and full of ideas, but had little experience in the matters of the world. As his thoughts weighed heavily upon him, he could hear the voice say again, *"Youthful strength will take you far and wisdom will be your guide through life's rollercoaster journey."* JT had not reached full adulthood yet. However, as the years moved forward like the rolling of film in an old movie camera, growth and development appeared and made an entrance into his youthful existence, maturing his knowing abilities. It was then that he was ready to put ideas forth that would work to better the lives of others who felt bound. Those that crossed his path would be helped. They would learn how to deal with the way things presently are.

"JT, are you daydreaming again? Boy hurry up, you have to get on the road," Grandpop said, eyes red. It was the next morning and he had awakened from his dream. JT was surprised to hear him say, *"you have to get on the road,"* because he had waited until the morning of departure to tell his dad the news of his plans to leave and wanted to explain why he had to go. Not made for small town life, he didn't fit in. Before he could start what seemed his soliloquy, Grandpop stopped him. *"What you rehearsed to spare my feelings; I don't need to know. You were always more like ya mama Etta, and I never understood you no more than I understood her, but I love you both, even if I wasn't as big on feelings. You understand young'n?" "Yes sir, I got it. You love us both."* Eyes cast downward, *"you know, daddy?"* J.T spoke those words in a tone of astonishment and expected his dad to engage in dialogue. When it didn't happen, he felt a heaviness in his chest, and tired eyes forced to remain wide open for hours, already burning, filled quickly with tears as he slowly raised his head to see his father's eyes wide open too, tears had formed in the corners of both Grandpop's eyes, but his chest no longer filled with signs of breathing. Barely functioning mentally, the rest of JT seemed paralysed too where he sat, Etta and Grandpop's baby boy stayed still as a corpse, there was only movement of eyes forward and then to peripheral and back again. Just like his mother Etta, his father slipped quietly away forever. Before JT could abandon him, he had the last word and moved on to eternity.

JT had not slept much in his childhood bed the night before

being that his mind was full of chatter, excitement, and dread. Throughout the years, Etta and Grandpop's bedroom was the one room in the house and world that he could go and find tranquility. Now, like the room, his mind was now eerily quiet. No friend of immortality, morbidity had found a place to reside where there were once healthy images and sounds. Within, JT searched frantically for chatter, but no words were spoken, no sounds were made of any kind.

As if on cue and with ninja-like skills, Aunt Ruthie stood next to him without notice or words. No longer needed to be many things to so many people, Aunt Ruthie's big brother, my Grandpop, JT's dad had broken free of his skin, his soul no longer entombed, but now free to roam the cosmos. Both Knowers, JT and Aunt Ruthie began reciting together the Lord's Prayer and Psalm twenty-three. Their voices carried into the other living and sleeping spaces in the little Jim Walter home. Soon other family members joined them in a chorus of reciting favorite sacred scripture and impromptu singing. This is what Grandpop would have wanted from those that loved him deeply and unconditionally. With their voices and breath, they honoured him for what seemed hours and each of them stood in a line, clapped their hands, and gave thanks and then finally, one by one filed in order by oldest loved one, passed by where he lay, bent forward and lightly kissed his forehead and afterward marched softly towards and through the bedroom door, turned left towards the kitchen and dining area.

Aunt Ruthie displayed the best skillets, pots, and baking pans, usually used during special occasions. While she cooked breakfast, Uncle Charlie used the rotary phone attached to the paneled wall in the hallway. Later, he told Aunt Ruthie that the basic funeral arrangements were complete. In two days, the free grave site for the poor would welcome the body of her big brother, the one who doubled as a dad too and knew her better than Uncle Charlie. The news of the funeral arrangements was sobering and the business and matter of fact of it had a sense of finality. Then the thought dunned on her that her new sister-in law, Grandpop's second wife, JT's stepmother was out of town visiting her friends and family and needed to be notified of her husband's untimely death. *"Where was that phone number? Charlie, do you remember where……oh I see it."* The number was on a torn corner of a brown paper bag, taped to the used refrigerator her big brother had purchased from a man who fixed old models and then sold them to families who couldn't afford new ones from Sears and Roebuck.

Aunt Ruthie and the stepmother had not become the best of friends, but they were always cordial with one another. Her big brother's second wife was guarded and careful not to get too close to her husband's little sister, but she knew that she had to have an ally or two in the family. Whenever she needed to feel free to truly be herself, she would take a couple weeks out of town where her family waited for her return. They had not imagined that she would have remarried nor married someone so unrefined. They didn't know her as well as they thought and there was more to her that meets the eye. She met the man that would become her new husband in the grocery store parking lot. Earlier, he let her cut in line at the cash register and they had smiled at each other. *"There is something about this man,"* she thought to herself, trying not to say it out loud. In town for a few weeks of vacation, they ran into one another in other places around the little community. The strong and silent type was her type, but she hadn't really thought she had a type. Divorced for a few years, she dated a little, but wasn't sure she would ever get serious about anyone else again. Meeting and feeling someone move into her heart surprised her. Mature love felt different than young love. It seemed that she knew what to expect and how she wanted to experience it in many ways. The only thing that she wasn't sure about was if she could date someone who was a single parent. When he asked her to marry him before meeting his children first and other family members, she was caught off guard. They met at the courthouse when she came back to town in the spring and were wed by a judge who seemed overjoyed to perform the ceremony and witness the vows. Aunt Ruthie and Uncle Charlie were the other witnesses. After the vows and saying I do, she felt a little vertigo coming on. It was actually nerves. The easy part was over. The hard part was facing the firing squad of school age children of various ages.

It was a day she would never forget although she tried really hard to. Everyone was staring as she walked up to the house's entrance. The little modest house was quaint, but not what she had imagined to be her forever home. The tour of the house didn't take long. Most of the house had been the living room and master bedroom with a private bathroom. The other parts of the house were significantly smaller in width that connected to a hallway bathroom, including a kitchen, and two tiny bedrooms. The six children watching her inspect their quarters, the small sleeping spaces crammed with bunkbeds, didn't seem very welcoming when making introductions. Their actions seemed forced and rehearsed. The moment was awkward and bizarre. The only children that she had known before were the ones in her childhood, and students who showed up to her first-grade classroom.

Becoming an instant mom was overwhelming. Outside of

herself, she appeared cool, calm, and collected. Inside she was having a conversation with herself. *"What were you thinking when you said yes to this man? You were not ready for this. Take it slowly is what all the smart people were saying, but you ignored their wise counsel. Smarter than the average bear is what you always thought of yourself. Look at you now. What are you going to do about those two older boys who made it clear that they don't want you around? Call Gladys, she'll know what to do."* Gladys was her best friend and always carried herself in a way that made one question whether she had lived on earth in another generation at least a hundred years ago. They had been best friends since elementary school. For as long as she knew her there had never been any problem that she couldn't solve quickly. She needed to hear her voice, but it would have been rude to make the long-distance call from the rotary phone in the middle of the meet and greet. Still wrestling inside with her insecurities and reality, the sound of her name being pronounced lovingly by her new husband jolted her back to the matter at hand. *"Yes,"* she said with her best fake smile. *"This is JT, my youngest son."* It was the same with all of the older children too. Each was told to step forward to meet her, but they didn't seem eager to be there. At the end, she was exhausted mentally and emotionally. She had better experiences meeting her students on the first day of school. It was a new start for everyone involved in the experience of first meetings and beginnings. Yet, it was the end of the old life that each person had been familiar with, and it was lost somewhere in time and never to be seen again.

    Meeting her new husband and then his family filled her memory and all of it was sadly too much for her heart. No one knew that when she went out of town to see her family, she made visits to her doctor who had told her that her heart like a clock was winding down to its last tick and that it was only a matter of time. She had thought at one time to discuss the inevitable to her new husband, but didn't know how to begin because she knew his health had become fragile as well. Which would leave the temporal world first, neither knew. Both expected the worst could happen, but expected a mustard seed miracle. The unwelcomed news from Aunt Ruthie was the tipping point for her own health fragility.

Aunt Ruthie waiting patiently to hear her reply to the news of the unexpected death, repeated the word, *"hello,"* at least ten times before hearing someone in the rotary phone receiver say that they were sorry, they needed to hang up so that they could call an ambulance. Still holding the receiver in midair and mouth half open, Aunt Ruthie just stared at Uncle Charlie, not knowing exactly what to say. After finally being able to collect her thoughts, she told Uncle Charlie what had just transpired. Later that evening, Grandpop's second wife passed on to eternity twelve hours after him. A strange thought occurred to JT His dad would either have two wives in the next place or they would all start over as single people.

Just as his dad and stepmother started their journey into eternity, JT was planning his next steps in the temporal world. It was a bittersweet moment, but it was his. He wanted his freedom, but needed his parents. He wanted to go find success, but wanted his parents to share in the adventures and challenges. Uncle Charlie and Aunt Ruthie had promised that they would be there as long as possible, and he loved them so much, but there still was a void. The emptiness could only be filled by those that gave him life. The suitcases would be lighter than the heavy heart filled with more care than anyone knew he carried for many years into his adulthood. His heart was a cracked windshield that needed to be repaired quickly before shattering into pieces or replaced before there was nothing left in its place. As a Knower, tragedy seemed to happen often, and he was helpless as an agent of change. Things just seemed DeJa'Vu more times than he could remember. Each time something happened, he would hear the voice first. It would warn him of impending doom or some form of prosperity that would affect him in some way or another.

JT's father's passing to eternity was unexpected as far as timing goes. The family had hoped that he would have at least another thirty or forty years with all that loved him so much. It's cliché to say that life is short, but it is truer for some than others. Nothing about Grandpop was cliché in any way at all though. His thoughts and everything he did were original in one way or another. Those that knew him well were astonished at the magnitude of his creativity. There seemed to be no end to what he could do with very few supplies and materials. Through anointed imagination, he only had to believe it could be done and put his hands to the many tasks and it would come to past. All the work of his hands was impressive. No one knew quite sure how many diplomas, degrees, certifications, and volumes of books and manuals it would take to amass all the natural raw knowledge he possessed. None of the knowledge was wasted. It was all used for good. The community could account for it and testify of it. Passing all of the knowledge on to his children was what he wanted more than anything in the world. Grandpop had always said that knowledge and understanding was worth more than any precious metal. That's why he was always encouraging and insisting that JT read. His youngest son was the last one to receive instructions of what to do with knowledge. As he watched JT in cap and gown and the paper being placed in his hand, Grandpop knew that his time was passing and JT's was continuing on to the end of a decade and closing in on the new one. In their own way they both had to go. Neither one of them would fit in that small town anymore. For both of them, leaving was a bittersweet moment, but it was one of those things in life that had to be done.

It had been thirteen years since Etta left to join others in eternity. The small town, family, and loved ones behind her, time on earth was shorter than it had been for Grandpop. Maybe she had always waited at eternity's edge to welcome Grandpop. Perhaps she knew that he would not be far behind her. He needed time to put their house in order before leaving their children and others behind. This all came to mind as JT sat near the donated grave site. The recycled wooden box sat near the dirt pile, waiting to be lowered into the ground. JT wasn't sure, but he thought he saw a dove flying above just as the preacher was saying, *"ashes to ashes, dust to dust."* Grandpop's corpse snuggly in the box had been given a final sendoff into the unknown for some and known for others. It was finished, the life journey on earth had ended. Sixty-two years of life were there and then gone. Celebrated for his altruism and talents, the earth and eternity would welcome him finally to rest. No more working from sunup to sundown. No more scooping out the poop in the chicken coop that doubled as a food pantry. No more hanging of the head in the presence of those who seemed to be and think that they were better than him because they had more of everything and none of the challenges and struggles, he experienced daily. No more worrying whether he was misunderstood or did the best that he could do for others and himself. All would be left behind, including foolishness, slothfulness, and the unconcerned and indifference of persons that he always failed to understand.

JT too would have to do a similar letting go. He would have to let go of the characters of his childhood drama that did not mean to do good by him, but would be good for his growth. He would leave behind those, including the religious folk and other adults who played a part in his seemingly early persecution. He understood and forgave them, but he refused to forget the lessons learned from them. Later, as a middle-aged man, he became more thankful because he had been freed from what had bound him before. He admitted that every now and then he felt some sadness and no doubt a little remorse for the childishness that ruled his heart for many years. With the mental fog lifted, he was able to see so much further behind and forward. His lucidity was a reason to celebrate each day of freedom from insanity. Peering through the Looking Glass of the past, JT saw what was lost on him as a young boy and through much of the developmental stages of his life, but once leaving the family heirloom behind to travel for many years, he lost time that could not be recovered. Sensing that Keila held the key to unlock the door that opened to the discovery of what was next for him, he wrote a letter to her, but addressed the envelope with her last known address.

The beating heart of Aunt Ruthie filled with joy when seeing the name on the envelope that she often prayed for three times a day. Keila just so happened to be visiting when the letter came through the postal service. She knew that JT's correspondence would come, but was impatient to receive it. She often thought that he went away too soon and that maybe she should have gone with him when he invited her to join him in an adventure of a lifetime. They were like twins. There were so many times when they would finish each other's sentences and laugh afterwards. There were also dark moments that could not be forgotten and left an awkwardness that stained their memories. As Knowers, they knew all that had to be known and any that was forgotten would be intentional if need be. Much of what they saw were riddles until they were not. All that was unclear became clear sooner or later. When they were together, they were better Knowers than when they were apart. Receiving the letter, Keila knew that it meant that she was needed, and that time could not be wasted. As her uncle use to be fond of saying, *"time waits on no man."* It waited on no one, no man, no woman, no girl, and no boy.

Keila loved her uncle because he kept everything real. There was nothing fake about him. What you saw is what you got. No mincing of words. Nothing, but straight shooting always. Great-grandmother had taught him well. He was to be the man of the house, the bread winner. They may have experienced what it means to be impoverished, but they were never destitute, the ship never lost as there was a captain at the helm. Through his hard work the family would always have a roof over their heads, decent clothes to wear, and never would be barefoot unintentionally. Everyone in the family looked up to her uncle and hailed him as a hero. After Keila's grandmother and great grandmother passed on to eternity the mantle of leader of the family was officially passed on to him.

As patriarch, the pressure and weight of the life he never chose for himself became greater. Although the life chosen for him was not his own to choose, he nevertheless without hesitation accepted it as a badge of honour. The responsibility to show others how to accept reality for as long as reality lasted was his to wield too. Being an influencer wasn't easy because sometimes accepting the fact that not everyone would listen was painful. Those that he loved most and didn't seem to understand how much he loved and sacrificed for them brought him the most pain of all. The last words spoken by Etta to him were that none of his words were ever wasted on those that he spoke to and especially those he loved most, and he would see that she was right. Those words broke him and affirmed him simultaneously. Etta's knowing abilities is what he loved most about her. One could say she used her superpowers for good. What drew Keila to her uncle was the softness that she saw beneath. Her Aunt Etta saw it too and loved him and pitied him too for it. Etta had once told Keila that her uncle would need her and her mama. The harder he loved the more fragile his heart became and JT was the only one that could not see it at first and until it was too late. JT was like his dad in that way. Loving hard was the only way he knew how to love. To live longer than his mom and closer to his dad's age, he would have to learn to love differently, with less wavering faith, and even less worry. Keila felt the heaviness in her heart warning that JT would fail in that area more than any other.

In his letter to Keila, he confessed that he had an *aha* moment. It was a moment of truth. The blessing of leaving home was that with everything past he could see clearly in the present. What he thought he saw before was just an illusion. In the time away, he was able to confront himself about the gravest of mistakes made in judgement of the one that loved him more than he could have ever known. Keila couldn't control the snuffling she experienced while reading the letter. JT was once blind, but finally seeing took her by surprise and Keila is rarely caught off guard. His knowing abilities had not matured as quickly as Keila's. A late bloomer, JT was becoming what Etta had hoped he would be when the time was proper for him to do so.

Placing the letter next to her heart, Keila sighed and then closed her eyes. Not long after, Aunt Ruthie walked over to her and kissed her forehead. She asked, *"did he say when he is coming?"* Without opening her eyes or moving any parts of body, laying perfectly still, Keila replied, *"in about a month or maybe sooner. It depends on how much overtime he works."* That part about the overtime needing to be worked, he didn't write and didn't have to because Keila already knew. Working and going to school was hard, but it was the way it had to be. JT didn't think about applying for scholarships and grants for his first and second year in college. It wasn't until his academic advisor had asked him how he was doing that JT said that he wasn't sure he was going to be able to afford the load of twelve hours that semester. Working thirty-forty hours each week barely paid for the necessities. The academic advisor helped him complete the Pell grant application and write an essay for a scholarship competition. In the meantime, he took on extra hours when they were available at work and later, he visited a military recruitment office after seeing an advertisement for military education assistance for those who qualified.

Keila had hoped he would stay close to their small town and attend the local community college in the county. It was no use trying to convince him to stay, wait patiently for the right season of life to move on to what was next and would always be there in the distance and waiting for him to arrive. It didn't matter that those others who loved him knew what he didn't know and wanted the best for him, he had to see for himself. Eager to go, he went and faced the challenges bravely and welcomed the opportunities. JT's big brother that was two years older than him, had told him that he thought that they would be roommates at least for a few years or throughout their twenties and was disappointed when JT declined his offer. It was probably for the best, being that not more than a few months later the brother two years older fell in love and moved his girlfriend in with him and not long after they had a baby together. JT did get three other offers that he had thought to maybe accept if he didn't leave soon after graduating high school to completely launch off on his own.

He first lived with his second oldest sister and then moved in with his oldest sister and later on with one of his friends from High School who had gone bravely outside of the small-town city limits to new adventures, promises of a better life and future. They did what he aspired to do and all fared well for all of them and JT was happy for them and longed for similar success. The little success at the beginning that he experienced was a little more than survival tactics.

He did what he had to do to live each day. Moving from other people's couches to finally his own room was the most success that he had experienced. The lady that owned the boarding house was very nice and cooked well too. She always asked JT how he was doing and that's how their conversations would start. He would say very little at first because he was an introvert. She seemed to like that about him. He seemed mysterious to her, and she was cool with that. With the other boarders, she was much more impersonal and all business, but with him she was different. Across from the boarding house was a building with tinted windows and the lighted sign out front had on it the name, Kat's Gentlemen's Club. In one of their conversations, she had asked if he had gone inside to check it out. She smiled and told him he should make sure he paid for everything with cash and that she would lend him some cash if he ever decided to check it out for the first time. He was surprised at her offer because he sensed that she was normally not generous. JT was interested in what was going on between them. His experience with girls was limited and his experience with women even less. Something was stirring inside that he didn't understand. Whenever they spent moments alone, he enjoyed the opportunities for small talk and what she was willing to teach him.

One day JT felt comfortable to ask, *"Would you tell me more about that spot?"* She replied, *"I would be delighted to, but are you sure you want to know?"* JT wasn't sure if he was ready for the unknown, but he was curious. He didn't understand why, but he felt both excitement and uneasiness. What he was feeling confused him. She sensed that she was right about what she saw in him, and it was attractive. Not long after then he would learn why. Gently grabbing his elbow, she suggested, *"why don't we go together Friday?"* JT was nervous, but he tried not to show it and so he said, *"cool."* She said, *"Right, cool."* Inside she was licking her chops, thinking about all the fun they were going to have. It would be like she was reliving her twenties! Friday night came really fast. It kind of just snuck up on JT, but it had not come fast enough for his landlord, the boarding house owner. The knock on the door startled him. He was finishing math homework. The voice on the other side of his room door asked if he was still cool about going out to the spot across the street. After hesitating for about a second, he almost stammered the words in a high pitch, but managed to say in his most manly voice, *"sure, yes, I'll be ready in a few minutes."* She hit him back with, *"ok, I'll see you there, I'm out."* JT looked down to see two fifty-dollar bills and a hundred dollars in one-dollar denominations slipped to him under the door of the room he was renting. Surprised, but a feeling of elation filled him, and some other things were happening to other parts of him that he didn't understand, but he kept his thoughts closely guarded. The words, *"to be young and foolish,"* kept coming to mind. He took a deep breath after buttoning his nicest shirt. In the mirror, he told himself, *"be cool. You got this. She likes you, that's all. Go and have a good time. Act like you know what you are doing."* Visibly shaking, he needed to calm down. Then he remembered that she said she had some liquid courage in the kitchen cabinet downstairs and to use it if he needed to. It was one of his many firsts, but it wouldn't be the last of his bad decisions. There was a dark side that he never imagined existed. It was his alter ego and his inclination to let the better part of himself be overcome and hidden beneath, that side of him grew and grew.

Chapter Six

Kelia knew before JT did what lay waiting ahead of him, but she could not intervene. Knowers are forbidden to interfere with what has to happen in free will situations. If he was cool with what he allowed to happen, those decisions and choices he alone had to own.

JT was honest with himself about who he was becoming, the introvert masked by extrovert characteristics. The change happened subtly and without preparation nor celebration of the liberation from the old self. It started with that first shot glass of liquid courage. The warm sensation and feeling of ease coupled with the quieting of the knowing part of himself. As long as he drank the spirits in moderation there remained a calmness about him, the edge had subsided. With that version of himself in control, he felt ready to venture into the uncharted waters of Kat's Gentlemen's Club. Dripping with confidence and a strange feeling of heightened expectation of pleasure that he wouldn't understand until later in the night.

JT had experienced some bad boy tendencies in the past as a teenager *smelling himself*, as the saying goes, but had only acted on them or gave into the impulse mildly and not on more than one or two occasions. The thought of what he did in the heat of the moment repulsed him, but he just couldn't seem to say no to the crowd that accepted him and his imperfections. He made excuses about where his head was at the time and that everyone was doing it. He thought about the illegal paraphernalia hidden in the boarding house almost in plain sight in the cabinet that was behind the door that made a crackling sound whenever it was opened. And he thought about the seeds pressed to the icy surface of the kitchen's outdated refrigerator model, flattened in between the cheap meats and green peas in the freezer part.

JT's thought process was interrupted briefly when the barely visible scantily clad slender girl told him to sit at the table in the corner not far from the swinging doors and where the smell of nachos and other fast food filled his nostrils. Once seated, he intently watched everyone and everything closely, surveilling the surroundings, the way uncle Charlie had advised him to do in new and strange places. At first, he didn't hear the girl speaking to him. *"Sir, are you ok, may I get you something from the bar?"* JT nodded his head, no, at first. His observation of the other patrons and the friendly service received gladly and naturally kept his attention. She said *"ok, I'll be back."* JT nodded his head yes as his mind seemed to temporarily return to an earlier time in his life when he experimented and let curiosity get the best of his younger self. It was the last time that he saw his dad with a look of disappointment, but to his recollection it was also the first time that he witnessed grace through his dad. Most of the time, undeserved favor would not be available, only his father's wrath.

Sitting nervously waiting in the living room for whatever would come, he remembered thinking, *"I should have gone through the back door instead of going through the front."* By this time, he was sorry for his sins but, *"mercy didn't seem to be in sight,"* he mulled over in his mind along with another million things that vied for attention from him. Fear had taken a firm grip on his faculties too as he sat in silence for what seemed like a whole eternity when the door opened, and his father's medium-built muscular frame walked through. He wasn't whistling as he walked into the room where his youngest son sat ridiculously fidgeting, thinking the worst would happen. There wouldn't be a smile and a *"son, give me a big hug,"* like he had seen T.V. fathers do, and he had envied those T.V. sons. Their fathers always seemed to be energetic, understanding, and compassionate. JT's dad walked with a bent posture because he was tasked with carrying the weight of the world. JT felt sorry for him at that moment and more than he did for his own self. His only plea was that his trial be started after his dad had rested and had a good meal. It wouldn't be good for JT if the handing out of punishment was done on an empty stomach. As his father walked past him with a half-smile, all his dad wanted to know was how JT spent his day.

Did you get any work done? He believed that idle hands were the devil's workshop. JT told him that he had managed to pull up a few weeds and with the motorless mower he trimmed the grass on both sides, back and front of the house before going to hang out with his friends. His dad didn't respond. Soon JT heard the creaking of the wooden foundation below the cheap linoleum floors in the hallway. His stepmother appeared before his father went to the bathroom to wash up. She looked JT over and without saying a word she went into the kitchen and put their stove top dinner over low heat and the cornbread in the oven. The smell almost made him forget about what he presumed to be his fate. He was hungry and felt almost faint because his stomach had been completely emptied of its contents after receiving the forbidden drink that would eventually become waste after making its way through the bloodstream, liver, intestines, and finally leaving the body which needed to recover from the effects of shock and borderline abuse. He thought to himself that he might as well get his strength back up while he waited for his trial to begin. As his father finished up in the bathroom, JT's brother, who was two years older than him and was attending community college in a nearby town, came in the house.

Seeing JT, he gave him an upward head nod. JT returned the upward head nod back and there was brief dialogue between the two comrades who had, for as long as could be remembered, fought side by side in skirmishes against the parental establishment. *"What's up man? What did you do this time?"* Briefly looking in his big brother's direction, JT, with a sheepish look and fake smile, retorted, *"You know, I do what I do, when I do it."* It was the same ole us against them back and forth and around we go again kind of thing, the struggle for power, equality, and respect never ending. They both laughed at the same time at the ridiculous exchange of words and the latter of the dialogue between them. The reply from JT made no sense at all, but it was his way of avoiding giving the real answer, revealing his guilt and shame, speaking in code. Shaking his head and taking inventory of his little brother one last time before going to his bedroom, with his back to him, he formed the peace sign with two fingers in the air and yelled behind him, *"good luck."* Under his breath, JT said out of earshot, *"thanks, I'll need it."* They didn't always get along growing up together, fighting for the same attention, but they shared the unconditional love inherited and taught how to use it by their mother, Etta. It would always bind them together like super or gorilla glue. His big brother had even taken the blame for some of JT's transgressions done in secret. The big brother thought that he might as well do what most of the family thought he was capable of anyway. JT's name was being called again softly and then again after nervous laughter. He felt a hand gently touch his shoulder.

"Excuse me, Sir, you ok, may I get you something from the bar to drink? Have you looked over the menu?" Looking up as if jolted back to the present, perusing the menu of mostly drinks and a few appetiser and meal options, *"Oh, yeah, sorry, I do, let's see."* His eyes had finally adjusted to the dimmed lighting in the cramped space designed to be filled with as many round tables and chairs that could be mustered lawfully, occupancy rules adhered too barely. It was also nice to be able to put a face with the soothing voice of the friendly, patient and kind attendant. The stringy blond hair underneath the layered light blue and green wig stayed hidden to not reveal her identity. It was a cool, cute, disguise to conceal the beauty without and within to the unknowing. A product of incest, for the last two years, she had been on the run from the backwards little community who had unsuccessfully tried to take land that they owned in the county and create a town founded for family members only. Legally denied within the court system the opportunity to file an application for incorporation, the very powerful family members fought any process of annexation to encroaching towns within the county.

Her story was interestingly dark, and it pained her to share any tidbits of its facts and the fallacies of patriarchy gone wrong. JT was surprised to learn that she and her partner of six months were tenants of the same boarding house that had taken in his weary soul not more than a few weeks prior to making her acquaintance. Most everyone at the three-story light brown building kept to themselves, all had a story that they were not eager to tell anyone, especially strangers. The attendant's partner was no different. She was misunderstood by her family who shared conservative views, and she swore never to associate with anyone who was close-minded. The first time she had an affectionate encounter with a girl, she liked it. No boy ever made her feel so comfortable and natural. She wasn't convinced that something that felt so right could be so wrong, unnatural. Her routine act at the club was anything, but routine. In the street and beyond, the news had spread quickly about the girl who came with a meal, a lap dance, and spoken word in a private room for VIP only. Rumor had it that she catered to high profile ballers usually, rarely did the low-income grace her presence accept on special occasions, birthdays, and bachelor parties. Her services were social, but not human social services in the governmental nor in the nongovernmental sense. The show was never taken on the road, preferred only in the private room of its gifted entertainer, the space seemed a magical dreamland for her patrons. Her work name and persona, Houdinia was the opposite of the vulnerable person she left behind whose name that could not be uttered nor revealed for any reason at all.

Houdinia was named Francis at birth. Her gender assignment was unclear until she was one year old. As a hermaphrodite, her parents knew she would have a difficult childhood and it would probably affect her socially as well throughout her life. Fearful that Francis would be shunned by family, church members, and peers, they decided it would be best to decide the gender she should be instead of waiting to give her a choice. The father had always wanted a boy, but figured it too risky to gamble on the wishful thinking that as a son, the child would behave with the expected amount of masculinity in private and public. Although, he understood that there would be no guarantees that the child would assume the natural tendencies of a human assigned the female gender, he felt comfortable with imagining his baby girl as a tom boy and that the world would be more accepting too and would more likely reject and taunt an effeminate male.

Houdinia recalled her childhood as difficult and confusing. Gender tampering was a taboo practice in which her parents felt obliged to carefully conceal from members of their religious affiliation and all family members and friends. No matter how strong the bond between them and those they loved and considered sharing their confidential personal information with, it had to be painfully avoided and self-discipline adhered strictly to. It was a secret they had to take to their grave, even if the stress of holding something so close to mind and heart eventually led to an early departure from their temporal life and into eternity.

Houdinia's parents died exactly two hours apart when she was a teenager, the year during which she had asked her parents for a divorce and not long after emancipation proceedings began. She thought it would be a win/win for all parties involved in the legal proceedings. Like many teens, she thought she knew everything, including what was best for her parents and herself. Proving that theory was more cumbersome than she could have ever known with the little life experience that she possessed. The realization set in as she saw her parents wither rapidly within months of her pursuing legal actions to desperately take control of her life. Although, masculine in many ways, the feminist within her clamored for attention and at time gained notoriety and then in one of those moments she chose, one perceived as self-preservation, she regretted what it cost her.

At seventeen, emancipated and an orphan, she avoided being ward of the state, but would also be disqualified from its support and benefits for minors. Self-excommunication from the church family followed as well, without any known provocation. As far as anyone in the medium size congregation and small community knew, Houdinia was quote, unquote normal and everything and everyone in her family were devoid of uniqueness and religious lawlessness. One of the things that stood out about her were her ingenious use of words on paper and in verbal recitation, similar skills to her doppelganger, an urban rapper and former dancer in a city up north. As leader of the church youth, she seemed more of a peace maker than rebel. Looks were deceiving due to the need for self-security.

Highly intelligent and resourceful, Houdinia had a strategic exit plan from her home written in her journal and ready to execute it quietly before her parents' demise. The obligation to keep the secret that hung around their necks and slowly drowned them in their continuous sorrow was no longer necessary. As she grieved the two people willing to sacrifice their happiness, peace, and youth in hope that she would enjoy all three valued purposeful ideals that brought meaning to their lives, a resentment for religious establishments took root and it would be many years past her youth that she would turn from her near hatred of hypocrites and the so-called pure ones.

Parts of Houdinia's story reminded JT of Uncle Charlie's brother's uttering of painful moments. A church musician, he had a similar experience, and he resented his parents for what he considered an infringement of his right to choose. It was what he called an unforgiveable violation that was of heavy consequence. For the rest of his life, he would feel the struggle for his soul, but even more so the struggle within to reveal both sides of himself, a dual story lay bubbling at the surface, but no gushing completely into the environment to be noticed by passersby or visitors to the worldly phenomenon.

His life ended in tragedy in a faraway big city where he thought he could live freely as dual gender and reap the benefits crossing from one side to the other frequently without consequence, living in the day as a man, but at night he transformed into one of the most beautiful creatures many men would say that they laid their eyes and anything else they dared too on. The hidden appendage was only revealed to those who were comfortable with the freaky side of nature and what the church people would call unnatural. Most lovers were surprised at first, but found themselves even more elated with the revealing of their own newly discovered sexual need for creativity in the dark and between the bedroom sheets. However, on one fateful eventful night, one potential new lover was unimpressed by the extra sexual organ. Repulsed and resentful of what seemed a betrayal of trust between consensual adults, without warning he blacked out and when he had awakened to consciousness a couple hours later, Uncle Charlie's beloved brother was no longer breathing. The emergency physician documented time of death was 12:05 am. The police charged the stranger with murder two, but the attorney for the defendant argued man slaughter and won the case because the mostly conservative jury had reasonable doubt about the alleged murder and believed that the evil act happened within the heat of the moment and because of temporary insanity. Uncle Charlie grieved for his older brother and best friend for many years until one day he didn't anymore. JT felt great empathy for Uncle Charlie, the disabled vet with so much sorrow in his past and maybe that's why Uncle Charlie only attended church services on special days of the year, Christmas and Easter. He had not been spiritually awakened nor had he desired it.

Every year the church that his wife, Aunt Ruthie and her family attended would serve as host of a church service that would last three days and two nights, Friday through Sunday. During that time everyone was expected to stay in church and not leave unless it was an emergency, or one had to go to work. Each family was expected to fast from food and drink. Some people would modify the fast to at least participate in whatever way they could. Charlie's brother-in-law and new wife decided that he and she and the children should fast half a day, deciding it would be good for them to have a spiritual awakening or an encounter with the unknown so that they would find spiritual knowledge of the Creator. To Charlie, knowing that his nephews and nieces were forced to seek the Creator was, in his words, not cool because they had no idea why they had to do something they were uncomfortable with, nor did they understand it. How would participating in something that they didn't understand benefit them, adolescents who didn't know God and questioned why He needed them to fast? That question would not be answered until later for Charlie and his nephews and nieces later in their twenties and thirties when all of them began to understand who the higher power, God is, and one of their brothers began experimenting with the non-prescribed psychedelics, but overcame his reliance on the substance.

In a support group for the drug addicted, the brother confessed if he could have understood sooner maybe he wouldn't have done the evil things he did while his parents were praying and soliciting their Creator for help, especially in desperate times. The sons were seemingly spiritually out of control and were heading down the opposite path and possibly temporarily detouring towards the right one, their parents could only hope. The brother often wondered if their parents ignored God when he was trying to tell them that their children simply needed them to show more love and attention. The devil was giving the attention-starved minors more attention than their religious parents seemed able to at the time. The generational poor struggled in so many ways then and were not exempt from the consequences of lesser parenting skills. The parents could easily see that they had needs that they wanted to be met by their heavenly father, but it was difficult for them to see that they needed to try as hard as they could to meet or see the needs of their own children.

Of the children of JT's father's church, many were close to becoming full-time members of the church of atheism. God was so distant to them that he seemed almost unreal and nonexistent. They learned before long to kick Him to the curb without missing a beat in performing weekly religious rituals. Although their parents thought that they had found The True and Living God; on the contrary they had found something similar and maybe even familiar, perhaps without trying to, they had made an image of what or who they thought He was. However, to their credit, the seeking for Him every day, especially on Sunday, Tuesday, Friday, and special church services was admirable and remarkable.

The children of the religious group learned to catch the Holy Ghost on Sunday night and lose the Spirit sometime between leaving church and going to school the next morning. JT's parents meant to bring him and his brothers and sisters up in the right way, they meant well in their doing, but it was not enough. Something was missing, a revival, an awakening or something else. The children craved what they thought was normalcy, a soccer mom, ballet, music, football, or any sports and arts programme would have been cool, as betrayed through television shows and commercials. To JT's father, all of that stuff was worldly and time spent foolishly. The Higher Power expected otherworldly experiences and wisdom from His children. To not see this meant that the person or persons were blind. JT didn't see church in the same way his father saw it. He saw church more as a place to meet people and show off your talents, but that wasn't the way he was supposed to see it. He just didn't understand church organization and religion for a long time. It wasn't that he didn't fear God. God wasn't even close to being the issue. Humans were the problem. Did God exist for the church or did the church exist so that people would have something bigger than themselves to believe in? Did He exist to scare people into forming a forced relationship with a Higher Power? JT was a curious agnostic for a long time until his personal awakening. The grown-ups didn't even have a clue how much he saw and heard during his spiritual sleep walking. Yet his father, one of the leaders of the religious group, wanted him to be like what JT saw as the wilderness wanderers and within, JT became more and more frustrated with the notion of what it meant to be on the right side of the history of religiosity.

Calling JT over to him one day, his dad said, *"boy, show me and the preachers how to live it!"* Caught off guard, it was times like that one that made him wonder if maybe he had misjudged his father. Maybe he was one of the grown-ups that did have a clue to what life was all about. JT saw their mistakes, but wasn't allowed to comment on or ask questions about those errors or missteps, being that wasn't a youth's place to do so without permission from the elders of the religious community.

But when his father made the statement, *"show us how to live it,"* something inside of him seemed to just click. He was alive with wonder. Wanting to sit down with an elder and just simply discuss life without judgement and being potentially shunned, he bubbled inside and felt he would almost pop or explode with excitement. Within him was a continual flow of energy, a mixture of emotional combustion, heightened sensitivity, spiritual, including the mental high which of all aforementioned, may be an understatement. His heart was open for the arrival and receipt of something, not sure what exactly, and his mind lay craving to receive from the giver of knowledge and wisdom.

It started happening more than expected. Unsure of what was going on he often sat alone, mentally in another world, a hypothetical one that was dissimilar and similar simultaneously, one that caused him to be in a peculiar state of mind. Alone is how he felt most of the time, but alone time is what the ninety nine per cent introvert side desired. He was the first to admit that he was so weird. He saw things that his family and friends didn't know he saw or felt nervous when speaking of those things. He understood things that they didn't know he did or wouldn't until later. And he felt the difference or gulf that stood between him and them and it didn't feel good to have this empty space there; keeping each of them from connecting to each other in a meaningful way. A void would remain deep within for an undisclosed time or for longer than he would remember. The feeling of emptiness in his heart would be exchanged for a more meaningful fullness, a mindfulness so to speak, when it would seem hope was forever out of reach and though not alone, the feeling of loneliness would be pushed out of bounds and into the abyss were all worldly lies, and ugliness was sentenced to reside for eternity.

JT didn't want to feel alienation for any length of time. But the realization that knowing didn't isolate him from the unknowers, did not materialise until later years. He had been afforded a gift that would benefit him over and over in the years to come. However, at the present time he needed to feel connected. The disconnection he felt to all the other life around him, including family and those he had befriended seemed more than could be handled by a Knower. The problem was that he wasn't as ordinary as he longed to be. He was a peculiar one, who experienced the extraordinary, but longed for the bliss that awaited in the ordinary. Someday, what had been complex would all be over. What was a birth complication exposed would be exiled as an outlier among the simple, the understood, the mature. Not born to be wild, but born to be free, in the temporal world with all the courage given to him to possess; the Knower was in a state of becoming who he would be in the distant future, a product of something bigger than himself; whom he had not fully come to know. Foretold by Etta, he knew as much about that bigger something as he knew about himself. Yet he could sense something near him, not quite in the shadows, but in between the light and the unknown. A higher being was calling that part of him that existed in thought, but deeper within. That was the first time he felt connected and wanted.

From that point on JT was no longer an accidental birth waiting to happen, but one that needed to happen. He grew excited in the realization that a being bigger and stronger than him, used immaturity to bring knowing to the unknowing and he was convinced that the world around him needed what they wouldn't understand at first. Tears rolled down his face for what seemed the millionth time, but that moment of emotion was different. He wasn't crying for that part of himself that had passed beyond the material world, his mother. He was crying to himself to rise. He attempted dialogue with himself through his tears. Learning to express joy with tears was something new for him. The song sang often in his father's church, "*I get joy when I think about what He's done for me*," seemed to make more sense to him at that moment and it marked the anniversary of turning from his past self to a better one.

JT's story of turning was similar to Aunt Ruthie's. It was an awakening that happened during a grappling with her sister Molly's senseless murder. The recurring nightmare of the tragedy ceased. It was as if a light bulb appeared overhead. She looked up and there it was, the light shining in darkness, and she knew its meaning instantly.

Uncle Charlie sensed that something had happened to his wife although he wasn't sure what it was, he could only presume that it was something happening for good to his wife and she needed it to happen at that moment and with preciseness. It would strengthen her when Uncle Charlie would be called away to the unpopular war to fight on the frontlines, knowing he would return, but unhappy that he had to go in the first place.

On his return to their life and children, she returned from darkness and their children experienced blessedness and a sense of normalcy again. The heaviness that weighed her in knowing that Molly would never return, would remain until the eleventh hour before Aunt Ruthie's death. One hour of peace would be her welcome gift from the One who created the knowing and unknowing. The same would happen for JT and Keila. Each of them would have a change of countenance. In the last hour their extraordinary youthful appearance would begin to fade. The sky would darken briefly. A slight tremble would be felt underneath the place they would lay. Etta's name would be sounded out slowly under their diminishing breath. The Looking Glass would flicker with images of their life to be, followed by life present, and finally their beginning existence. The loss of them would be felt around the world. International Knower's flags would fly half-mast for a month or until the mantle was passed to others, novice or not in the way. One of the three would receive the Nobel peace prize posthumously.

The gift of knowing was never taken for granted and felt more a burden than blessing. The lowly who received it were esteemed, but felt unworthy the rest of their lives. The high born who felt it thrust upon them were humbled, but valued their new wealth more than their old inherited station in life. Born of the former, JT knew the strangeness that came with the gift, but also the feelings of elation and the belonging to otherworldliness.

When they were in high school, Keila and JT had often discussed the fine line between imagination and real paranormal activity. At the private university, Keila's published doctoral dissertation on the study of the effects of spirituality and religion on mental health and its value to science was praised for its original thought and Dr Keila was awarded a research grant to continue a study of the subject. Meanwhile, JT was being self-educated first in a homeless shelter, and then a boarding house and night school where he met others who struggled like him with having an overwhelming knowing ability. They were all late bloomers. All would joke later that it was better late than never, for those that needed to process a spiritual awakening and transformation that could only come by way of an out-of-the-body experience if not an in and out-of-the-classroom one.

A continuation of JT's late blooming happened during the year the Gulf War began and ended briefly. Unlike the unpopular war that Uncle Charlie was forced to participate in, the Gulf War received willing participants only, except for the lawless who were given two options, go to war or go to jail. A few months after the war, the truce was violated, the skirmishes began again.

A similar bus and plane that brought Uncle Charlie home from conflict in a jungle in Asia carried JT towards a similar one in the Southwest Asian deserts. It was unfair, and at the same time the U.S. military display of shock and awe was impressive. The grunts closer to the frontlines of the action either never lived to tell what they saw or were forever changed by the horrors played out over and over when they slept and during experiences of phantom pain near the sight of their amputations while back home with family or in a VA Nursing Facility. Some of these soldiers JT knew from basic training and others he met briefly at his first duty station after completing advanced training.

When he finally touched down in the arid climate, witnessing an unusual warmth, and buzzing of large flies swarming the tents that dotted the native landscape, while he moved with purpose to the barking orders of his platoon sergeant, JT's long legs stumbled across a barely visible ½ pint milk carton as he with great care held onto his sand-coloured duffle bag. A touch of brain fog affected every soldier, who had boarded the plane and landed twenty three hours later. As they received their shelter assignments, they welcomed a place to lay their heads and burdens down. It wasn't anything like home or the ritzy hotels in America, but it would be enough.

He and the others were permitted to rest until seventeen-hundred hours. The mess hall would open and serve them at seventeen-thirty hours. In the meantime, in a meditative state his consciousness processed his need to explore a world old to others, but one that was new to him, and then before long, his short attention span was interrupted, he heard his name being called back home to the small town that he avoided like a plague, but always revisited in his imagination.

"JT, are you finished already? No, Mrs Mulan," he replied. He lied to his second-grade teacher because he did not want more brainless toiling within the boundaries of his tablet and notebook. Robotic action seemed to take place as he pretended to write along with the others in his class. Like prisoners on a ship that employed slave labor to move its large mass across the ocean, they went through the motion as well as any labor force of school aged children. Schooling was a necessary business that grown-ups systematically involved children in with very little allowance of creativity and self-realization.

Reflection, often confused with day dreaming was what he liked to do most often than all other things; he found it quite liberating. He could not express enough the freedom it brought to those among his classmates who endured hardships beyond their control. Comparing reflection to chocolate or other delights would not do the mental activity justice. It is more like never making a mistake out loud and having people look at you strangely of thinking outside the box that students are caged. Or it was like doing unique things that you loved in private without being laughed at for being weird. It was comforting to think things through because it was not the same as carrying out an action that may be seen as good, bad or not cool. Philosophizing wasn't allowed and the popular saying, "study long, you study wrong," was accepted as a mantra. Unfortunately, a love for philosophy was an important part of being a Knower. Before Mrs Mulan would make her rounds again and check for in-class worker stragglers, a disruption in the classroom happened. A clanging sound seemed to be coming out of a brown wooden box located above the door, below the ceiling. The children were told to leave the classroom quickly by columns. It was the third fire drill that grading period. Every student filed out through the classroom exit one column at a time as practiced.

JT was the last one in line and as everyone was walking briskly down the nicely buffed tiled hall lined with portraits of important people on either side, their shuffling feet tapped to a familiar beat and surprisingly stayed in sync. Before long, a voice inside of JT's head told him to look behind himself. Turning just in time to see someone and one of the cafeteria ladies coming out of the head custodian's corner office was a very peculiar sight to behold. The cafeteria lady's hair net was halfway on her head. The curls and brunette streaks were more noticeable than before. Ms Wilma had always seemed a little different, but then again adults were always doing something or another oddly. Yet there was something about her that day that was more odd than usual. Why was she coming out of the head custodian's office? As JT turned the corner he saw the office door open again. Not knowing who had come out bugged him. It was like missing a scene on TV because someone accidentally or purposely turned the channel.

He was a nosy one and most children he knew were too. It is the number one thing that got him and his friends into trouble back then. His friend's mama's sister would call any person that was nosy, a nosy Rosie, no matter their gender. She would often say, *"Get your big nose out of my business!"* Getting into people's business, windows, and a lot more was a big problem in JT's neighbourhood. He knew a lot about what he shouldn't have known and learned even more from a young age until he was old enough to vote against immorality alongside the rest of the self-righteous. Staying out of the business of worldly folks was hard to do, but he couldn't help himself. He had to peek and pry. Wanting to know seemed harmless. Before eight, he had learned from his big brothers to investigate within bedroom windows and listen beside walls for sounds of endearment and mating rituals being performed within earshot. Late at night he would turn the TV on to enjoy the adult entertainment furnished through stolen cable where the same touching, breathing and joyful encounters were witnessed. At that time, he was most mesmerised by the strong female type, especially the brainiacs of all ethnic groups who were adventuresome and creative in acting out the loving with their whole self, emotionally and physically.

He often fantasized about the touching that happened in the private lives of the cable television stars. *"Private move it!"* The time had gone by faster than he had realised, and he was embarrassed about where his thoughts had taken him back in time.

Chapter Seven

Like Zombies, his platoon moved through the mess tent line. The brain fog had not subsided. One could debate that it was a symptom of jet lag or possibly a side effect of mandatory vaccinations against the new viral, bacteria, and fungi strains that awaited the brave military personnel in the foreign country, where their enemy could be visible under microscope only, or as well as by the naked eye through the M16 rifle scope when the absence of desert sandstorms and swarms of seemingly mutated large flies permitted. Airborne enemies sometimes snaked through fighting spaces as well and compounded the challenging conditions of the battlefield in the strange land.

On the other hand, the middle-eastern culture seemed a powerful reminder of the simplicity meshed with complexity written of in textbooks and travel guides. Recognizing the spiritual overtones of the religious culture near the battlefield, and a sense of purity, and modesty displayed by the local people, JT felt shame that up until present, he had lived the opposite of what was meant by righteousness. After visiting the chow hall and being dismissed from the final formation that evening, he went and laid down, feeling wiped out from the day's events. Soon, he was fast asleep and experiencing rapid eye movement, a good sign of sleep health. In a dream, he saw three people standing at the top of a sand dune. Each spoke to him one after the other in three different languages, but all said the same thing. The first person spoke in Arabic:

التعليم لا تنس ابن البلدة الصغيرة والخالق. في قلبك ، يجب أن تحافظ على كل وصية من أمك وأبيك" الأرضيين والأبدي لسنوات عديدة سوف يطيل عمرك ليجلب لك الهدوء والازدهار. لكسب الرضا واسم خاص في نظر الله والإنسان ، اربط الحب والإخلاص في كل مكان حول رقبتك ، وشم على قلبك حتى لا يتركك أبدا".

The next followed in Greek as the previous person was finishing the message: *"Διδάσκοντας μην ξεχνάτε γιο της μικρής πόλης και τον Δημιουργό. Στην καρδιά σας, θα πρέπει να τηρείτε κάθε εντολή της επίγειας μητέρας και του πατέρα σας και του Αιώνιου για πολλά χρόνια θα παρατείνουν τη ζωή σας για να σας φέρουν ηρεμία και ευημερία. Για να κερδίσετε εύνοια και ένα ιδιαίτερο όνομα στα μάτια του Θεού και του ανθρώπου, δέστε την αγάπη και την πίστη γύρω από το λαιμό σας και κάντε τατουάζ στην καρδιά σας έτσι ώστε να μην σας αφήσουν ποτέ."*

The third paused and then spoke gently, but with authority in JT's native English: *"Teaching do not forget son of small town and the Creator. In your heart, you should keep every command of your earthly mother and father and the Eternal One. For many years they will prolong your life to bring you tranquility, and prosperity. To gain favor and a special name in God and human's sight, bind love and faithfulness all around your neck, and tattooed on your heart so that they never leave you."*

JT awoke to the barking of more orders and a feeling of freshness and mental clarity. The chow hall, the makeshift dining tent would be soon overwhelmed by famished military troops. Grabbing a few baby wipes, deodorant, and fresh underwear from the duffle bag branded with his last name. He quickly worked on cleaning the essential body parts while still in his sleeping bag that perched atop the foundational cot that served to suspend in air and support the sleeping bag and sleeper, both successfully avoided contact with the sandy surface and occasional scorpion visitor beneath them.

In less than five minutes, JT was fist-bumping with battle buddies outside of the bunk area where some soldiers were standing in awe of the sunrise. An officer walked by, and each were jolted in time from their trance to salute respectfully his rank, signified by the butter bars that reflected the sun's rays. Afterward everyone in sight doubled timed towards the mess hall where each would receive rations called MREs. There seemed a mad rush to stand in a long line to receive prepackaged, ready-to-eat meals. JT hoped to receive his favorite, a Louisiana style jambalaya meal. Instead, he received his second favorite, chicken and rice, pound cake, crackers, and kool-aid. He would need the one-thousand calories because it was true that the Iron Man platoon did more before 8am than most civilians did the entire day.

He felt a hand on his shoulder as he began to inhale the last morsel of morning chow. *"JT, my man, what's up boy?"* Before he could answer the 205 pounds of nothing, but muscle corporal, the adhan made its way through the air over the designated military camp area. The chaplain that flew over to the strange land with the platoon had given the soldiers a crash course in the native culture and included a lesson on the native prayer time that was to be respected in the presence of the native people. The adhan was heard through a microphone and speakers and seemed to be assisted by the wind and transported for miles across the barren land to believers in the strange religion and to others that might be persuaded to convert to what was believed to be the true way. JT heard a voice say, *"Trust in truth that only comes from the One that knows the origin, the beginning and end. Give your whole self to him and he will show you the true path. The Knower knows and increases in knowledge that is not of self."* His shoulder felt a stinging sensation. Then there was a slap against the same shoulder and then laughter as JT looked up to see the corporal looking at him strangely. *"What, why you looking at me like that man?"* JT could only stammer the words. The corporal slapped his shoulder again as he questioned whether JT should go to sick call at the medical clinic to get checked out by the Army physician. Still in a daze, JT was once again transported to a different time to his younger self.

His house was a couple of blocks down and so it didn't take long for him to get home. He took caution as he opened the door that he didn't let it swing too wide and that it did not slam shut behind him. In addition, while coming inside before letting the door shut, he had to yell, *"Motha I'm home,"* to his stepmother in case she was in her room or somewhere in the back. One time one of his brothers forgot and came home to find her in just underwear bottoms that he and his big brothers called big draws or big girl panties. His brother was so ashamed in that moment and repulsed at the sight that lay before him stretched out on the floor in the backroom in a meditative state. She didn't know he was even there. He slowly and quietly backed out the door as if he had not seen anything and had just arrived home. Opening the door, he yelled, *"Motha I'm home,"* louder the second time. Down the narrow hall, there was scrambling, panting, and shuffling of feet. Soon, he heard her yell back, *"Lord, boy don't you come back here!"* When he told JT about that incident, he and JT laughed until their sides started hurting. That was so funny and later when they were grown men, they would recall that moment and laugh again until it hurt! After that day, she made it clear to the boys again that they better never come into the house ever without shouting a warning that they were home. That was fine with them too because they did not want any stomach-turning surprises either.

Well, that day JT gladly shouted the warning that he was home and somewhere in the house. She shouted back that she had heard him come in. Now that they both knew one another's whereabouts JT could try to make his way back to his room where a place of sanctuary awaited his weary soul. He felt worn down from all that had transpired during the course of the day and the activities that filled it.

In his travels around the back of a neighbourhood filled with Hud houses and plum trees that dotted the landscape along the back streets that had mostly potholes and that meandered into a graveled road that only one car at a time could drive across with barely enough space to avoid the eroded land next to it that was known to swallow cars whole when out of control drivers were forced from the road into what at first looked like crevices under each wheel that sank into the unsuspected crater that subtly appeared out of nothing. Mysterious happenings related to new abnormal and paranormal adventures seemed to always be there waiting for JT and others to embark upon with earnest and ponder the significance. Each one brought him closer to the realization that he hated his life even more each day and that its meaning was questionable in the fishbowl he called home.

The adventure on that day had to be the worst thus far. The older kids of the hood did a lot of stupid stuff and the younger ones got caught in the middle. That day, JT literally barely escaped and was alive to tell the story. It was a little secret game of *"devil meant"* as his father would have called it. Although he made it out alive, he was still shaking with fear and anger. It was the first time that the older kids had included a double barrel shot gun in their game. The gun was pointed at

JT's head, *click*, and then it was pointed past him towards the corner of the house near the window, *pow*!

"Private, are you ok? What's wrong with him?" The physician could see that JT's eyes were open, but he could not get him to respond to the sound of his voice. Two soldiers from his platoon had used the technique called the fireman's carry to take him the length of two football fields to the hospital tent. It was the gun shots of a skirmish in the far distance that sent him first into akinetic catatonia and then comatose later in the week. It was settled that JT would have to be flown to Ramstein Air force base in Germany for treatment and recovery. It was unknown to the platoon sergeant, the second lieutenant, and the physician that he was suffering from a PTSD from the childhood abuse suffered at the hands of older children who themselves were traumatised by their own abusers who were older children too. It was a generational curse over the neighbourhood and the children of each generation hoped to escape its victimization. Only a few would physically leave it all behind, but none would emotionally and mentally completely escape the nightmares and the daily prison they were held captive in until their last breath on earth. Each could recall what seemed a shadow and coldness that followed them no matter what distance away from the small town that they found themselves. Over and over, they felt afresh the dark incidents happening to them. It was cruel and unusual and almost like being stalked by someone who was gradually a stalker, then predator, and finally serial criminal.

The harassed, preyed upon, and victims of serial crimes dared to tell only the few that could be trusted about the continuous torment of their past, present, and fear that their future would be negatively affected or in jeopardy too. Data showed that each of the few, also known as the brave ones felt a calling to the military for reasons that would not be made known until years later. None of them would retire from service, but all went in and transitioned out after four years as honourably discharged military men and women. They shared the same experiences and job specialties. Each returned to the place where they entered military service as disabled veterans.

JT went back to the boarding house across from the Gentlemen's club. The disability check was enough for him to live in the room and receive his meals downstairs with the other tenants that he jokingly, but fondly called the family. The property owner served them three meals a day and seemed comforted to have the company residing under the same roof.

She had not seemed to age from the last time JT had seen her. They had become friends although she was ten years his senior. Their relationship had always been platonic and using the Gentleman's Club as a classroom she taught him about women, but there was one tender moment when she got the news that her mother had died, and she needed the comfort of a friend and lines were blurred and nearly crossed. Fortunately for her and JT they took a step back wisely from doing what friends chalk off as regrettable and a moment of weakness. JT's sympathy and compassion were felt as deeply as would be by any empath, and she was overwhelmed by the flood of emotion that swept through her to the depths of her soul. When he confided in her about his mom's passing and how young he was she collapsed in his arms and their noses touched as they both wept softly.

The transition from military life to the comforts of the boarding house felt natural. Unlike Uncle Charlie, he wasn't a draftee uprooted from all he knew involuntarily to fight in the unpopular war and welcomed home again as a hero to some. JT was a volunteer soldier chasing the GI Bill and he hoped he wouldn't have to kill to better himself with technical training and some college. It seemed that the genie of southeast Asia had granted his wish. He escaped with his life intact, and the brighter days hoped for within his grasp.

At the boarding house, he was with family although not with those who were blood-related and knew him best. Uncle Charlie and Aunt Ruthie's position in the family of blood relations had changed due to the passing of his father and mother. JT's older sisters and brothers accepted their aunt and uncle as head of the family much easier than they would have their stepmother. Aunt Ruthie was her big brother's favorite sister and Etta's favorite sister-in-law and Uncle Charlie treated Aunt Ruthie well. It was settled in heart, mind, and out loud that all was as it should be. The blood relations were at peace and the former heads of the family were at rest. Their lives seemed to be going in a preordained direction. Yet, JT kept coming to various family members' minds because of the emotional and mental fragility that was present within him and noticeable by those that loved him deeply.

At fourteen, he had confided in his big sisters and brothers his escape plan. They started watching him closely from that point until the day of the inevitable family intervention that followed a Divine one. It was out of desperation that he thought to end it all one or two ways because without clarity and peace, only two options seemed available. He felt he had to either chart his own path to the other world or self-disappear into a place on earth no one, even the FBI, would be able to locate his presence. JT was at an age when kids like him started to wonder more about the who, what, and why of life and sometimes become something that they didn't understand. JT had not met a male Knower, someone that truly understood him and being understood mattered. After Etta died, very few people understood what was most important to him, especially the Knower half. What was crucial at present was the knowledge of the male Knowers to come, those that would mentor him and those that would be mentored by him. Up to the present, he relied on the females who understood him and knowing as much as they could about his past, and present, but very little about what lay in the near and far distance for him and those he befriends and loves.

Aunt Ruthie had kept her promise to Etta. She was always available to JT whether he thought he needed her or not. At times she smothered him with what seemed like too much love, but it was her way, and it was the way that she and Etta were most alike. The way of the Knower was as noticeable as the crucifixions on chains that hung low around the necks of believers in the One God. Sometimes the precious things that remind believers of their purpose and the meaning of life lose their symbolism and importance for one reason or another because things sometimes happen and are unexplainable. It's the mystery of it all that's hard to accept. Whether acceptable or unacceptable, some things can and may be accepted without much argument. JT could argue that analyzing one's own predicaments and experiences was tiring, but needful. Tenaciously, he picked or took apart what made him the unique person he was led to believe he was. Needing to know was important to him because he liked understanding himself and life in general. He knew that people like his kindergarten teacher, Mrs Kindleson were similar to him in thought and like him had gotten the urge to dig around for information that points to the origin of some fact that they desperately wanted to prove or disprove. Sometimes facts are found to be what they are, the truth. *"Disapproving of truth was not the same as disproving it as theory or an informed guess,"* was the thought that came to JT most often.

Truth was captivating and it held his brain, mind, and heart in a dungeon without a key that would open to clarity sometimes, but on other days it led to peace of mind and that was all he needed. In a continued wrestling with truth, a male Knower would help him someday, but it was difficult to wait for that day. His dad, big brothers and Uncle Charlie had limited capacity for knowing and could only provide minimal assistance in JT's life-long quest to know as close to what was and is infinitely possible to know. Even before the family intervention and the Divine one after, his big sisters were desperate to know him better and how they could help him become what Etta knew was possible. Aunt Ruthie and Keila too felt at times helpless and clueless about JT's needs. As two Knowers, their vision seemed narrow and short. There were times when they couldn't see at all because either there was too much light or not enough of it at all and many sleepless nights followed their bouts of Knower inability or sub-ability, not lower ability in a sense, but more like incomplete in ability when it came to knowing male Knower relatives.

Keila first noticed the phenomenon when JT left home at eighteen years old, but the sub-ability was always there, but would not manifest the four years prior to him leaving. A darkness was blocking much of her adbility to reveal the knowing. It was the low hope beast that had followed and marked the family for at least three centuries and this was known because of surviving family historical records and all other family records before then were lost. It wasn't until sophisticated medical tests of the brain were discovered to accurately detect the presence of the low hope beast that high hope surfaced. High hope was sustained after the discovery of mental health treatment to end the three centuries of dread.

Keila remembered that the rearing of its ugly head that fateful year was a reminder of the curse and with it came a blessing too, one that reminded JT of his duty to and place in the family. His impatience to go and become could have cost the family the blessings that would come later if his premature escape plan from small town life had not been delayed. Meanwhile, another dark vicious monster, the cancer beast, had come to claim his father and would only give the family four years to prepare for the inevitable. The fight for his life would be short. The final battle would inevitably be lost.

If the doctor's prediction was true based on the family history, JT would be the cancer beast's next victim. For the next thirty-nine years, he would do all the knowing that was possible for one person. Keila wept. for her favorite uncle and her favorite cousin because it was the one thing that she could know during that dark time. Aunt Ruthie was the only one who Keila knew would understand and they wept. together because they knew that favorites were like first loves, you only get one of each. There would be no other favorite big brothers and nephews for Aunt Ruthie, nor would there be any other favorite uncles and cousins for Keila. The anxiety that they both felt in that single moment was immensely more than what was felt during their Charlie's disappearance in the jungles of Vietnam.

Etta had prepared Ruthie and Keila for the fateful day when both death dates would come. She reminded them that all lives had an expiration date and it's what we all do with that knowledge matters. Ruthie and Keila knew that Etta was right and that events were set in motion from the beginning of any of their lives and it was up to them to do what they were obligated to do. Call it a gut feeling or intuition, it was what it was, and they knew that they couldn't waste time being sad. Time was precious and they had to spread the news about life and its abundance and where it comes from and what everyone should do with the time that was left to each person. Everyone would hear, but not everyone would listen. Truth tellers throughout the history of the world felt the obligation to tell of the inevitable eventful experiences that came, happen, and would continue to later, even if all that was foretold, telling, and told long ago fell on deaf ears. It was the Knowers' duty and they accepted it. In fact, something was planted inside of them long before they were conceived and swam in their mother's amniotic fluid. Genetically speaking, Knowers were made through means that only the Creator understood, and although not of the world of humans, yet always connected to humans through usual and unusual ways. It was always believed that the connection wasn't always known through words too, but at one time it was known through feelings and symbols only. Words were not enough and using them to connect to the Creator was foolish because of human ineptness in deep communication and whether as Knowers or Unknowers, they were even less capable of being adept and astute in receiving the connection and seeing its usefulness and value. Knowers were created to bridge the gap between the Creator and the Unknowers.

Knowers were never superior in any way to Uknowers, far from it, but just chosen to carry an almost impossible burden. The Unknowers had to help carry Knowers, reminding them of the bliss that existed in the midst of turmoil, chaos, and pain.

Etta's husband was assigned to her, Uncle Charlie to Aunt Ruthie, Keila's mate to her, and JT's partner to him.

Before any of them were married to those that would carry them, they had Unknowers in their family or those that were friends that would carry them until they tied the preordained proverbial knot. It was hard to be friends with a Knower let alone married to one because their moods were unpredictable. There was always a seesawing between elation and deep sadness at least thirty per cent of the time and one or the other could tip to one side without warning.

All Knowers at some point in time would have to be aided with psychiatric or spiritual care or risk becoming isolated from other Knowers and Unknowers, family, and friends. Other Knowers were persecuted for being different. With circumstantial evidence, others were prosecuted for crimes that years later would be proved that they could not have committed. Empathy for Knowers wasn't witnessed too often. To not be accused of being a Knower lover was the path most taken. To have one in the family or to marry one was usually unknown or pretended to be unknown. There was an activist that had a dream that it would not always be that way and that there would be a day Knowers and Unknowers would live openly together in understanding, collaborating to make the world a better place to live.

The military was the first to allow integration and interconnected marriages between the two unalike groups of persons. In wartime, the two unlikely pairs of comrades were linked through common fear and hatred of the enemy pointing weapons towards them. In basic training, Uncle Charlie heard whispers of a Knower in his squad, but the drill sergeant had warned all soldiers of the don't ask, don't tell policy. In the trenches they would all need each other. Each would hold the other's life in one's hand. Just as predicted, each would be comforted that whether Knower or Unknower, they would be friends against a common foe. In some cases, the mate of a Knower would lead them and bring them safely home to their unknowing mates, family, and friends. The camaraderie would be for the battlefields on foreign soil, but once back home all would face the reality that awaited them. The feelings of trust would dissipate, and all would be as it was before the war and the short-lived understanding. The truce was over and new battlelines drawn in the real world. Even years later after the nation's first Knower President who was openly married to an Unknower, little would change in the hearts and minds of Knower haters. During wartime, only against a common foe would the nation stand together. Division was the beast that marked the hearts and minds of haters across the proud nation. It would eventually inevitably be the cancer that eats away at the souls of the fearful, of the misunderstood, and the progressives who were driven by the need for speedy development and self-aggrandized maximizing. Knowers were the champions of knowing for good and proponents of minimalism for balanced living. One thing that most all Unknowers innately knew, the day was coming. Knowers would one day be the majority. There was a common fear among Unknowers that a reckoning could follow, or compassion and empathy could rule the day.

If Unknowers could only see that they didn't have to force things to go their way. It could all go the way for all equally. Many had lived with inequity for so long that they didn't know any other way. When each began their own life journey, they didn't know how to live life fully and in the way the Creator intended his creation to live. *"Show me how to live it,"* were the last words JT's father had said to him, but how, was the question that was pondered over and over again at eighteen. He searched for a long time in the hope of finding the answer to how to live as a Knower. There were many who lived as one of many types. Although it would be a long time before they would feel free to leave the closet and reveal who they were, they always stood out in the world in a comfortable hidden identity.

Many learned early on to hide in plain sight as leaders, inventors, innovators, the less known wealthy, athletes, creatives, members of secret societies, corporate and government movers and shakers, as well as fraternity and sorority brothers and sisters, etc. The world community of Knowers have always been a diverse group. Not all have been known to be good, but usually not intentionally bad either.

While volunteering with a nonprofit group that advocated for prisoners who were denied mental health services, JT met a Knower in prison who claimed to be in the wrong place at the right time when a crime happened and because he was behaving strangely, he was taken in for questioning, charged with the crime, a jury of his peers read a verdict of guilty, and he was sentenced by the judge within a few months. At first, JT thought to himself about the saying, *"everyone in prison is innocent."* Yet, he couldn't get the man and his story out of his mind. Getting too involved with someone else's life drama, especially a Knower, was not what JT had wanted to sign up for. He started feeling like he was in the wrong place, but for the right reasons and needed clarity or a strong drink first, then a good night's rest and then clarity would follow the next morning if he was lucky.

His head space needed clearing first before he could help someone else, especially a Knower with their own head space clutter. Frequenting the night spots or after hour questionable social venues helped JT to quiet the many voices in his mind, but when the last call for alcohol was made, he was no better off than he was before the security person welcomed him as a sober regular. Senses dulled temporarily, the voices would return the next morning, accompanied by a pounding headache and the sobering reality that he had behaved foolishly once again. The desire to be a boy scout eluded him, but each day he promised that as long as he had breath in his body, he would do better than yesterday. The desire to do better drew him to groups who were doing good things in the community and eventually to a prisoner who said that he didn't need anything in particular from JT, but just wanted to feel connected to someone that seemed familiar to him, a Knower.

"What would Etta, Aunt Ruthie, or Keila do," he questioned to himself. At that moment, it became clear to him that doing wasn't it. The prisoner didn't need him to do anything. The prisoner wanted JT to just be himself. Whoever he was to his family and friends, the prisoner wanted that person to show up in visitations in person, and through letters, and phone calls.

JT remembered reading about the many undesirable people who were imprisoned and put in concentration camps across occupied Europe during World War II. For many of them there was much about them that was unwanted by the society in which they trusted and desired to live among. Treated with disdain due to the suspicions of unscrupulous characters, who said they witnessed unsubstantiated claims of misconduct done in the community by those that they held prejudice against.

When history or the stories of before in the time behind the present has been forgotten unintentionally or on purpose, the future is put at risk. A better future lay ahead for the generations that remember what matters most in a community.

Knowers and Unknowers will always have to put in the work that is critical to community building to prevent the tearing down of the beautiful community the present inhabitants have been afforded and should be privileged to maintain and improve whenever possible. Too often the generation after the previous one develops a lapse in judgement due to memory corruption in human computers. When the brain fails to compute the obvious, the human machine becomes dysfunctional. What follows individual dysfunction is group dysfunction, whether it be a family, a gang, or political party. The building blocks of corruption and dysfunction are sometimes noticeable and ignored, but sometimes the seeds of either or both planted in society are subtle hints stemming from disagreements that brew into something else. When the dark clouds gather in the sky, common sense beckons everyone that is uncovered or protected from the elements to find shelter, a pavilion, or car port. The storms of life come and go and come again and again, but wisdom and learning the lessons through the experiences gained from them is not a given for some. The prejudice grumble about the personal, professional, and political storms that follow their individual or group's bad behavior, but often fail to make vital corrections to past mistakes as well as listen well to and apologise to those they knowingly have injured in anyway. JT's prisoner friend welcomed the lessons of life, but hoped to avoid the unpleasantness that comes with some of them. He talked a lot about the things he would do if he had a do over.

"Man, my life has been an adventure and full of events, JT I wish I had paid attention to the little things as much as the big things, the prisoner confessed unexpectantly. Seeing that JT was a good listener, the prison leaned forward, eyes narrowing. *"How old are you? You seem older, but that's just the Knower part of you. I'm guessing you got to be no more than twenty-six and some change."* JT taken aback by the shift in conversation, but jolted to straighten his posture in his seat to listen more intently to the next sentences as if he knew something, a piece of a puzzle or confidential information, data, or intelligence that was about to be secretly passed to him. The prisoner continued, *"Dude, you're helping people like us, but who's helping you? I'm worried about you, bro.,"* was the prisoner's poignant last words, before the guard yelled, *"times up,"* to the visitors. It felt like JT was back in the Army and had been punched in the arm to get his attention and bring him back from a distant place in a daydream. In a zombie-like motion, he followed single file the visitors down the sterile hallway and listened to the doors of check points that would soon be locked down for the rest of the evening. It was true what the prisoner had said, however inconvenient it was. Somethings are important enough to pay the necessary attention to. JT needed someone to listen to him too. Who would listen?

Getting people to hear the silent screams is almost impossible. Listening is the gift that few possess. One is usually trained to listen. Once a person is trained to listen; they may use this skill to pursue education, jobs, relationships, etc. Many children have wished that parents would listen in a meaningful way, see their experiences through their eyes and understand with a child's heart. The fair, dark, brown, yellow, tan, and all in-between skinned have worn a look of despair and distress from time to time. They are in streets of major and minor cities and walk the roads of counties and country sides. Crying out in silence, no one hears because it is convenient to close our ears and pretend to be deaf to their cries and screams for help. The crying becomes loud and is heard clearly when people open their ears to hear. However, not knowing the cries exist, the sounds muffled or muted, it feels better to those that wish to remain ignorant of its annoying and compelling platform from which it speaks. How can anyone resist its call to action? The silent screams use several platforms to speak from: illegal drugs, nicotine habits, alcohol abuse, emotional disturbance, etc.

Various addictions including alcohol abuse may be named among the vices that plagued most Knowers. JT questioned why they were allowed to take such a grip on the lives of the vulnerable? He found comfort in the bars, the clubs, the secret gatherings, the reunion with friends in the dark. Together, he and other less desirable people felt a sense of wholeness. Apart from that, they were undistinguished pieces scattered across the cosmos, not belonging to any group, anywhere, misunderstood, and pushed to the margins of society.

Without a good listener, Knowers easily become loners, hitchhikers, and hermits. Feeling discarded, not wanted, they haul themselves off to the social landfills. Once there, they settle into a certain obscurity. It is a kind of intentional unknowing that undesirables become known for. Not making it through life, they fake happiness until the end of their existence, usually a short one. It is an accepted fate, lives stolen in desperation to escape a real internal and sometimes invented external persecution. The prisoner had seen it too many times and educated JT on the different realities and fates of Knowers.

As prisoner and eccentric, he had once told the prison psychiatrist that everyone is a little crazy. He smiled and then after thinking about the statement deeply, he laughed. The psychiatrist told him that he was right and that in his opinion the prisoner was normal. Either the man of science and medical doctor was agreeing that it was OK to be a little crazy or that acknowledging that one is somewhat crazy means that the person has the ability to see that there are degrees of craziness which indicates that the person is not very crazy and may function pretty well without being put on some type of psychotropic or hospitalized or both. It felt good to be affirmed in the normal parametres of the mental health state. While growing up in New York City, the prisoner had met some pretty interesting people who may qualify for a few treatment programmes at a local mental institution. He jokingly told the psychiatrist, *"if your business slows down and you need me to throw some your way, I know a few people who could use your help with understanding their reality or lack of this reality that you and I opportune."* Listing the characters from his childhood and adult memory wasn't difficult.

Chapter Eight

In the prisoner's old stomping ground there was a funny older character who injured himself as a child when he flew over the handlebars and landed headfirst on the pavement. From that day on he suffered an affliction known as photopsia. He was nicknamed Astrologer because the stars were in his eyes and he went around declaring to all who would listen, *"it's time to go to heaven."* It was hard for any person young or old not to laugh and tease him about the oddity of arguing over something that most people in the community could care less about, but cared more about the day-to-day struggles which included traveling from point A to point B and back to point A. Traveling to heaven would never be on their bucket list until later in life. Yet, Astrologer would argue this point to all who would listen. Sometimes, some of the children would get him started by saying, *"Astrologer, where you going?"* Poor guy, he didn't have a chance to give a serious reply to their insincere inquiry before all would be holding their sides because it was difficult to hold their laughs in. The prisoner remembered how he used to try hard to keep his smirk from becoming a grin. It was just impossible. The other grown-ups would get so angry with those children for mocking this adult that seemed and looked like he was an alien, an immigrant just passing from any of the heavens above and would return as the malignant ocular tumors spread throughout his occipital lobe. But he wasn't alone in the twilight zone that many of his kind called home. Sprinkled throughout the borough were neighbours who resided near where the prisoner had once lived and were just as odd in their ways too.

One of them, Birdie was flighty and like a mother goose, she made sure that her nine younglings followed her in the same manner as goslings each day to the nearest bus stop, taking leave of the minimally maintained twenty story high rise that was barely federally funded. There were gentrification talks for years, but like its residents the neighbourhood improvement project was abandoned. Birdie babies' daddy's disappearance after number nine was born almost broke the mom completely, but it was that youngest one who she named Angel, who saved her. At least that's how Birdie's own mother, the nine's grandmother remembered it.

Before meeting her demise, she had a dream that one day Angel would lead her mom, brothers, and sisters out of abject poverty. As the ninth in line following behind, on the day she, her mom and siblings took their daily stroll to the nearest bus stop next to the community playground, something happened that would put her on a path to a personal destiny. Across from what her brothers and sisters called the fun spot she noticed a man with just a towel wrapped around his waist and midthigh area, walking by with his head in the clouds. Momentarily, he looked her way and nodded, while pointing up towards the puffy white cotton balls in the sky. Tilting her head up and then sideways, she witnessed it too. *"The heavens, one, two, and three,"* she squealed! The unusual adult nodded and then Angel and he, Astrologer burst into uncontrollable laughter.

Another character from the borough, New Adam lived as freely as any sub-human life form and many of the citizens in the tight knit community treated him in the inferior way most peculiar persons are treated. The butt of jokes was just part of the small stuff that he endured for as long as he could remember. *"Naked,"* he would tell people he came into the world and naked he would prefer to walk around in it. Down the streets, he was found prancing about on sun shiny days. Not caring who saw him or his peanut flopping about in midair stride. The men would turn away in disgust, except those that enjoyed the view and encouraged him to do his thing. Most of the women were embarrassed, but of course others jeered or cheered him as he walked the streets with no sense of shame. If any children needed a visual lesson on human anatomy; they certainly received one that day. Not a child anymore, but perplexed and feeling a little childish in his mind about what he saw and its traumatic effects on him, the adults and especially the underaged, the prisoner questioned the insanity in life. *"Why did madness exist? Why must it continue."*

Questioning was not unusual for the prisoner, who was always curious about the why of things except the subject of his curiosity was close to home. *"Why did this man do this, embarrassed his family? Why was he allowed to? And why does God allow anyone like this person to be born?"* He wondered if his uncle, the one that was called New Adam had any idea what his family was going through while he led what seemed a carefree lifestyle. Obviously, the prisoner could not see what was happening in his uncle's mind and if he did, he would have known that there were no ideas, just continuous conscious streaming of disconnected data. There was an awareness of the data, but the ability to connect it all to make sense of the reality his family faced each waking hour of the day was impossible. Cheap help was sought from community activists/politicians. Talk was cheap and they had plenty of it to give. The promise of change sounded good, but real change was bad for the business of politics. The mentally ill person who had no family or whose family was only valued if they voted, had no hope or low hope, which translated in any language to absence of power and negated equity among peers.

It was the wealth of knowledge that the prisoner desired because with it came power and some veracity of equity. If available, it was what his family needed lots of, to do more than survive. For many years they expected power to come from any actual or at least apparent loyalty to religion. They were incorrect and would never be rewarded for wrong thinking. Their thinking of God had to change if they wanted to experience the authentic nature of their Creator and the only One that could offer them true and genuine transformation, leading to something better. The clock was ticking, a rethinking of politics outside and inside the Church institution had to be recycled and renewed to be used during their lifetime and if they achieved better, their discovery could be passed down to the next generation or if the opposite became true, their children and possibly grandchildren would inherit a generational mess.

The prisoner had wondered about a lot of things outside of politics and religion that affected him and his borough, but the latter of those two important players in cultural and community life left the impression that was the most indelible. Politicians disappointed him, but preachers of the gospel were not gaining favor at the moment either and were falling further behind in the popularity race.

For many years, he longed to understand the church down the street which held the membership of New Adam, but had failed him and others of that fold by not allowing them the comfort of refuge, but instead denied him and them the access to a safe space, the pew and mourning bench, financed with his family's tithes and offerings. Was it necessary to usher him back out into outer darkness where ridicule awaited his seemingly accursed soul? The way in which the prisoner had always been more curious than amused at the sight of the lowly creature, New Adam, had stayed with the prisoner for as long as he could remember. Not just because New Adam was family, but there was something about the man that evoked empathy from the prisoner for other reasons that he could not explain. Only one time had the two locked eyes, but during that moment words were not exchanged in dialogue, but in effective monologue.

New Adam stopped in his tracks for a little while to speak clearly to the prisoner's younger free self, one sizzling summer. It was hard to forget the record-breaking number of senior citizens in the borough with only fans to cool their homes who suffered heat strokes and if they were taken to the hospital, many never made it back home. It was in that same dangerous heat wave, the two would meet. They were both walking on a sidewalk that you could fry an egg on, and it was next to a street pothole being repaired by city workers earlier in the day, their activity cut short due to the crew not able to bear the increase in hot temperatures. The cones, and signs made it impossible for the two men to avoid walking close by one another in passing. Without warning, New Adam grabbed the arm of the young man he had seen through his peripheral vision often watching New Adam being put in an ambulance or police car and being the entertainment of the neighbours. Looking the young man directly in the eyes, he assured him, *"it's ok, I was banished from the garden of Eden, but it won't be long till I return. Eve will be there too."* Caught off guard by the words and the sincerity in which they were spoken, the alarmed young man pulled away, nervous and fearful of what the peculiar man, his estranged uncle would do next. When thinking about it many times over later and in the present, he felt shame.

He wondered about his community and its ability to be the kind of place that helped those in need. Most people either seemed selfish and self-important or just didn't care enough about others to do something self-less. No wonder his father was looked upon as a modern hero within a community that experienced the same tragedies of the past again in the present and was on track to see them return in later years. In the concrete jungle only the strong survived and without help many of the indigents would not.

Some called him a saint. With supernatural patience, his father helped people like the father's older brother New Adam find the resources they and he desperately needed. With encouragement, some of them became better, stronger, and survivors. Later, someone from another generation would come along and reveal the next step in their evolution.

In the meantime, the prisoner's father would continue his work, the calling he felt was his cross to bear until it wasn't. He was a worrier that would die of a heart attack, but not before passing the mantle of his work to another. As a Knower, he was always trying to help other Knowers, especially the male ones. His son, the prisoner, had always admired him for that. Everyone else in the borough seemed to think highly of him too.

In a letter, the prisoner asked JT to visit his father and mother. *"I know that you may not want to be in a place where it seems that everyone has trouble sleeping and is always in a hurry to go nowhere, but you are needed there. I can feel it."*

As JT read those lines a second time, he paused again to ponder the meaning behind the words. JT had never felt needed before and it stirred him inside. Self-Help Gurus, and self-important people came to mind. Their messages were the same. People who needed them flocked to their side, and stood in long lines and crowded rooms, pregnant with hope. Each believed that their patience would be rewarded with at least a sign of things to come, a token. None felt deserving of anything, but the crumbs of life, but all knew that so much more existed and was available for asking and receiving. All longed to become important to others and secretly they needed to feel the importance that attracted power to them, and they to it. The commonality that surfaced often in their minds and hearts was the fear that plagued them. Soundness of mind was desired, but brokenness of heart arrived instead and remained if fear extended a continuous invitation. The gurus were Knowers who misused their gifts. Indifferent to the problems they caused when supposedly helping those who had generational troubles, other Knowers genuinely empathic to the burdens of various weights carried by those who needed the help that they could offer, rescued the troubled at great cost. The families of the latter Knowers felt a sense of pride to be their kin, but a deep sadness and anxiety too due to their predicted short lives. Their heroes could only bear the burdens of and for others in a short length of time and if they did not pass the mantle to willing Knowers who felt the calling and knew the risks of accepting the calling until the end in life or death, their end would come sooner rather than later.

Never considering himself a hero, but someone with a chronic health issue, JT was a worrier like the prisoner's father. The prisoner knew after meeting JT that he had finally understood why his path had been chosen and why prison was just one landmark on the path. Neither talked of it, but both knew that their friendship and meeting was not by chance, but was part of a grandeur plan. There was something glorious at work in both their lives. As JT wrote his reply to the prisoner's letter, another correspondence was being sent on special paper that had letter head, officially releasing the prisoner from his months' long confinement. A doppelganger, the real criminal had been caught, detained, and he confessed to the criminal act.

The law-and-order Unknowers had finally protected and served, righted a wrong and a little more was right in the world. The newspaper headline was more about the increase numbers of doppelgangers in the known world and less about justice for all that are innocent. In the south of the nation, there were many more injustices that needed to be made right and although in the north the numbers were less ambiguous in quantity, they too were worrisome to Knowers like JT Another thing that worried JT was that he would not be able to stay out of the limelight that came with helping others.

Soon, he would be thrust into the everyday of what it means to be a part of the big city life. The awful traffic jams, with it the impatience manifested by the honking of horns of every type. There too would be a symphony of other sounds, some evoking a pleasantness and others not so much. As a Knower, what awaited him was bigger than he could have imagined. Smaller stages existed in sparsely populated towns. The denser the population the bigger the stage on which he was expected to stand and show himself worthy of the work given him to do.

Research of the areas of the largest city in the nation needed to be done as expeditiously as possible. The decision to reside and where was best for him was usually a challenge in any place he chose to visit or live and the difficulty of it quadrupled due to the size of the city area in miles. The other thing that grew in size and heavier in weight was the worry in his heart and on his mind. Thinking of what lay ahead caused great consternation. The perturbation was followed by exhaustion. Unintentional intermittent fasting was self-prescribed for those moments of physical and emotional ailment. Naturally, meditation coupled with fasting gently and carefully carried JT down the path of healing, but not without some consequences. With his breathing and brain activity slowing to close to nil, life signs were concerning. If found in the catatonic state an ambulance may be called and he did not want nor needed that kind of attention. Intentional fasting of any kind was avoided, if possible, but intermittent fasting was of less consequence than longer fasting because of the difference in time span. Yet, some fasting was necessary if only to bring clarity to the season of his life. What was more important to him most, was the necessity of reappearing to the group downstairs where they awaited his presence in the dining room.

Yet JT lingered longer to take in the present moment and the past experiences before taking the crucial step towards future endeavors. A breath was taken slowly and breath out with intention. Every part of the sparsely decorated and furnished room had significance. Nothing through his eyes was overlooked. On the cracked, flaky eggshell painted windowsill was a full grown plant. It started as a seed planted in rich soil in a dollar store purchased coffee cup. It reminded him of what was true of himself. He too started as a seedling in that room before sprouting into a mature upshoot after being cultivated in the richness that life offered in the boarding house and surrounding community. It was as if he was being called and led to a place he would know as home for a few years. Everything that he needed seemed to be in the centre of the downtown area and the downtown was the centre of the entire city and the centre of the sparsely populated county was the city. The boarding house, barber shop, Gentleman's club, at least five worship centres, a used car dealership, a bakery, a homeless shelter, ethnic restaurants, two convenience stores were squeezed in between high-rise buildings that held the secrets of the wealthy and powerful. Hidden behind those buildings and two blocks down was the bus station, important to the broken American dreamers and dabblers in the black market.

JT remembered Uncle Charlie's story of riding on a bus from the military base back to their small town and he always romanticised what it was like to share its cargo space with strangers. He laughed to himself when thinking of the ridiculousness of his youthful thinking of something so ordinary and necessary to those who could not afford a plane ticket or were afraid to fly and hated driving long distances. Reality set in less than two minutes at arriving at the small bus station in his small town and the experience became even more real when his small suitcase was put below the bus among the rest of the cheap stuff that would be insignificant to those who possessed the best that money could buy. Far from luxury it was unlike the coaches that were outfitted with the best technology, sleeping quarters, and kitchenettes.

The smell of old cloth seats stained with unidentified substance and in between them were sometimes found unused cloth diapers. Underneath may lay a small precious metal or paraphernalia of various kinds, legal and illegal. The coveted seats were those perfectly assigned to the middle of the bus. The back seats could be the worst or the best depending on the passenger's situation. Military veterans enjoyed the anxiety relief the back seat offered. While others with stomach and bladder issues preferred it for obvious reasons.

While during the long ride many suffered in silence the children let it be known to all adults that they would not bear the humility and discomfort quietly. Relief from their screams and whines came midway for JT when the bus stopped at a connecting station and the brave single mother of three slowly exited and received one large suitcase shared by she and three little boys one year apart. As the family walked from the back seat to the front each adult nodded respectfully to the single mom, put something in her hand, and told the children to be good to her. Though all were strangers to her they were familiar in different ways with who she was, where she had come from and where she was headed. She was one of them, a bus person. It wasn't something she asked to be, but because of unfortunate circumstances it was what she became. If she held her dreams together tightly and passed them on to her three boys maybe she would experience something beyond what was her life in that present moment.

JT hoped for her sake that she and her three little guys would see brighter days ahead. In the meantime, he closed his eyes and enjoyed the comfort of silence in those remaining 40 miles. At the next stop the feelings that would surface would be bittersweet.

The house and home that was familiar to him would seem halfway around the world. Yet, it would be close enough to return to as much as possible with access to affordable transportation. The money that he had saved working part-time at the local grocery store while he finished two years of high school would not last long in the slowing trickle-down economy in an urban dog-eat dog fast moving environment and so he agreed with the voice in his head to be sensible with spending and if need be resist the urge to be prideful when considering a return to small town life.

His big sisters had schooled him on being worldly wise and they were always real with him and sometimes their G and PG Rated conversations and discussions led to Rated R questions and answers. They warned him of the prideful young people who waited too late to return and became victims of scams and associated with crimes and criminals. Others turned instead to drugs and alcohol and were led down a dark path of addiction, violence, and prostitution.

His thoughts went back to the bus and the single mom and her three boys. He wondered if she learned those lessons the hard way instead of listening to the experiences of those older and wiser and who wanted better for her. Inside, he examined himself and promised to listen to his better Angels and know when it was time to return home and then relaunch into the bigger world outside his smaller one on another more appropriate day.

The plan that he had journaled in the summer of his High School Junior Year was to think like a survivor and someone with good behavioral instincts. He wrote down the basic things that would be necessary for him to live. Food, water, shelter, clothing, and air were at top of the list. Growing his vegetables and buying cheap stuff would work. Drinking the water from the faucet instead of buying the fancy bottled kind would help too. He was willing to stay at the shelter, but the lady at the front desk told him that the boarding house owner was a friend, and the lady was sure that something was telling her to refer him to her friend for affordable lodging. The kind lady sent JT off with a brown bag lunch and a bottle of orange juice and there was a paper inside the bag of food that had emergency social service sources, including a thrift store. As he took in the air around him outside of the shelter, a feeling of elation filled him.

The basic necessities were checked off his list. The boarding house would provide much of what he needed daily. Still the sadness of leaving loved ones behind competed with the happiness of taking his first major step into a new beginning down a path that he seemed destined to walk. There were very few Knower nomads, but he was one of them. This was one of four big moves he would gladly and nervously welcome into the story of his short life. Boarding and military housing would satisfy most of his single adult life needs. Both would be left in the past when the end approached.

JT hadn't told anyone that he was leaving for the second and last time and if he would ever return or to at least visit his first adult home away from childhood home. The first time he left the boarding house and his friends behind, he was mourned by those who had grown to know him and were noticeably close to him in their heart and his, like family. As a Knower with a worrier and warrior's heart he was always troubled and alert to the madness that threatened the souls of every Knower and Unknower, emotionally, mentally, and physically.

The seeds of the future war on terrorism of all kinds planted, he had been called towards the battlefield, its native soil, although he believed that he was being led to greener pastures by way of basic, and advanced training as a soldier and the promise of higher education once he had met his obligations to his country. Surviving the overseas conflict, he returned to his blood relations and the friends who were like family, but only for a short time.

Again, he was being called away to a no lesser training ground with no delusions of what was at stake at the end. His drill sergeant, a Knower had seen better days and many battles, but was older than the average worrier/warrior Knower. This time, no barking of orders, with gratitude JT would be welcome to join an elite member of a fighting force that very few knew existed in the world. As he sat at the table, through his peripheral vision he looked over each person that he had for a few years broken bread with. They had watched over him as he had them. The honour to do so was a pleasure to all and each of them showed it in the way they treated each other. The corners of JT's eyes glistened as he became intensely aware that their communion that day was one of the last, they would have as a family brought together not by blood, but through mutual understanding and respect. The unconditional love that existed between them would never be questioned by them or anyone that knew their bond. The preciousness of relationships such as theirs stood the test of time and absence. Their hearts would hold the memories and the feelings that lasted a lifetime. None would take for granted the season that they were afforded for as long as they could be together.

At the head of the table usually sat the owner of the boarding house, but she invited JT to the honoured seating. Each bended back straightened and molded against the chairs while their legs enjoyed the open space underneath the vintage Chinese Carved Rosewood dining table. What they had just witnessed was unusually a first for all of them, even the one that had resided and dined the longest within the walls of the two-story Victorian house.

There were twelve bedrooms and so naturally there sat twelve chairs for twelve members of the family. One of their daily meals was served at exactly twelve o'clock noon. The doors of the house were locked not one minute past twelve midnight.

JT's chair was considered the twelfth chair because he was the last to arrive and it was pulled away from the table until he returned from military service. No one quite knew how the owner of the boarding house knew that he would return, but strangely she did. She possessed an unusually high hope regarding JT's return. In his letters to her, he had not hinted that he would be back. In fact, his intention was to go back to his hometown to spend a few months with Aunt Ruthie and Uncle Charlie. However, plans have a way of changing for whatever reasons. He wasn't sure why they changed, but he knew that purpose was the cause. The flight to and from overseas gave him a chance to think through what mattered to him. The long trip was similar to those taken by bus passengers. The seat space was just as cramped, but without the discomfort and awkwardness of sharing the space with a third customer. Nor were there seat assignments, but each were taken first come first served. The window one was the best seat for thinkers, day dreamers, readers, and writers.

At the bus station, right before he bought the ticket, he felt and knew that he had to go back to the family in the charming residence. It was five hundred miles in the opposite direction. He wondered to himself, *"would I be welcomed back? Would my chair be empty still?"* What he didn't know is that until the final goodbye, there would always be a seat at the table for him. Only he could give it away to another who needed it as much as he did. The contract between him and the owner of the boarding house was more than just written words and signatures binding them in honour, truth, and law. Mysteriously, something else not of the natural world meld their minds and hearts from far beyond the cosmos. There was a force within and around her that drew him to her and a kindred magnetism that both pushed and pulled them together and finally apart. Neither spoke of it out loud. Each thought it within their brain. The mind and heart held it for safe keeping.

JT and the boarding house owner were kindred in spirit and thinking. He was the male version of her. Their connection wasn't quite like the one he had with Keila nor Aunt Ruthie, but there was a link.

When the two first met, it felt as if they had known each other their whole lives. Although of two different generations there was commonality. Also, not to mention, there was something as deep as the soul within JT that draws those that have commonality with him to them.

Etta had noticed the charm of her baby boy when he was born, and it had grown by the time of their encounter with the fruit at her bedside before their final goodbye. That supernatural force was powerful then and she could only imagine its propensity for immenseness in affection and effecting of others who became attached to JT None would know this more so than Mrs Kindleson, his Kindergarten teacher and then the boarding house owner and later his wife.

All that he had affected and attached himself to were never the same afterward. The strangeness of it was that something seemed to bounce from them to him as well. It was unintentionally quid pro quo. Each needed the other for short and long periods of time. Nothing creepy nor perverted ever happened between them and him. Nothing was ever needed that couldn't be given. Unspoken contracts were already in place before each physically met. Some were Knowers and others were Unknowers, but the commonality was the magnetism. On meeting for the first time, it was like the meeting had been ordained in a time much older than the present one. When the Knowers met JT, it didn't seem like coincidence. It was like looking in the mirror and seeing one's own reflection. The startling discovery that others exist was sometimes more than could be handled in one setting. The event was usually a historical one of remarkable magnitude.

To have twelve sat at the same table for any number of years was not heard of very often. They all knew that they were of the same fold and followed the same way. When one would leave temporarily, the chair was removed from the table and placed in the corner. If it was understood clearly that the fellowship had come to an end and the Knower would leave with intentions of never returning, the chair would remain at the table and a white cloth would be placed over the back of the chair until another would take the place of who was referred to as the last sheep.

JT was experiencing what was known as mid-transformation as he sat for the last time at the Twelve's table within the walls of the Philia's Boarding House. The others had already transformed completely from sheep to shepherd. What they were before was in the past. Their present was quickly becoming the past too. Each was warned to never think about the future and if it came to mind, let the thought slip into infinity. The only shepherd Knower that this was harder for than most was the worrying shepherd, Knower. Knowing this, JT delayed his journey to New York City for one month. The eleven would train him and help him finish his transformation. Moving forward to the next mission without finishing the cycle could prove disastrous.

The trick that needed to be learned as well as humanly possible was the coupling of the brain and heart. The vital organs would have to work perfectly in congruence. Knowing and feeling would have to be in sync without fail consistently twenty-four hours per day and seven days per week. The ability to sustain JT's life was literally in his brain. Whereas the control of emotions and the power to be happy lie in the confines of the heart. Misfiring of electrochemical signals was not afforded. Neurons had to communicate properly without fail. Malfunction of the brain could correlate to less than ideal Knower behavior.

What is suitable and appropriate could be misinterpreted and the Knower would no longer be recognised as a person of calling to mission. Although one is more than his or her calling, it is the calling that gives purpose to the one called. Mental health and mental illness are closely tied to the health of brain and heart or lack of healthy brain and heart functioning in harmony. When there is a malfunction, nervousness rears its ugly head and the appearance of too much of it is a sign that anxiety is not far behind.

JT had experienced as a teen both normal anxiety that aided his knowing skills and the high doses of it that clouded his knowing effectiveness. It was also the cause of the bleeding ulcers that led to frequent severe stomach pain and because the family had to choose between his dad's cancer treatments and his self-imposed affliction, his ailment was triaged appropriately and handled with prayer. With the plaguing of his emotional suffering, the importance of completing his transformation from sheep to shepherd could not be overstated. It could mean the difference between a good life and debilitating mental health.

As an adult among his extended family he received uncommon attention to his mental health needs. The link between the group was so strong each could feel the emotional pain of the other. JT was in good hands and his family back home in the small town didn't have to worry as much about him weakening mentally and falling victim to the madness.

The individuals that made up the team of twelve were drawn together for this purpose alone. Each came to fulfill the grandeur plan for their lives. Knowers and Unknowers would profit from their completing of the cycle. It was a late coming of age, but better late than never. Late blooming benefited Unknowers more than Knowers. Because Unknowers understood barely the concept of time, their awareness of its use was lacking to say the least and they wasted most of it on studying the stock market's weaknesses, others worried about systemic ineffectiveness, and how to get ahead in life and ahead of every person they knew that had entered the rat race, the one race that no one would live long enough to win.

When JT's father finally understood the concept of time, Etta lay barely conscious before his eyes. With tears streaming and a feeling and knowing of clarity that he had failed to experience before, he whispered to her, *"time waits on no man or woman."* With one last gasp of air, one decimal above a whisper, she concurred, *"indeed it does not my love."*

JT's extended family of twelve understood that time belonged to the Creator of all that existed on earth and beyond. Its measurement was like all human-made inventions, it served man's advancement. The will of the Creator was rarely desired except to serve humans' vanity, a selfish purpose again and again.

Knowers and Unknowers were once lumped all together as the guilty as charged in their conquest to worship the best of themselves, often referred to as gods. The Creator had become the myth in stories told over time, first verbally, then through written record. Soon many former worshippers of the Creator became cynical and skeptical, no longer the believers they once were. All were becoming lost in their own imaginations, never regaining a true sense of reality. Generations never returned to claim their spiritual inheritance. The love for false and fun things and procreation became their two reasons for living a supposedly fulfilled existence. The substance that could bring them joy beyond the temporal world was sought less.

The nonmaterial power that lay within Knowers lay dormant for decades. It awakened within a few in the early twentieth century. They formed the first twelve and hid who they were until it was safe to do so. Each still agreed to wisely use their skills and gifts sparingly. None of them were sure how their families and friends would receive who they had become. Friends and associates could possibly become fearful of them and behave strangely towards them and their loved ones.

JT remembered the stories Aunt Ruthie told him and Keila when they were old enough to know the truth of their origin and their purpose for being alive as the end of a century was drawing closer. More and more Knowers were becoming of the age to take action as it was known for a long time. The modern phrasing was knowledge maturation. Postmodernists began to coin the phrase, existential transformation. In any case, the school of thought premised that whether Knower or Unknower, everyone on earth was in danger of extinction. Herd mentality was driving many of both groups towards a steep cliff to their inevitable dangerously downward movement. People of each group were endangered species. Their fake evolution would lead to real consequences, their long fall from grace.

Keila was the first of the two young Knowers to interrupt Aunt Ruthie with questions. She possessed one of the keenest minds in their small town. *"Mama why doesn't the Creator destroy everyone and start again? It would be easier for Him to do that than for an outnumbered bunch of loosely confederated foot soldiers to push his agenda. I'm not questioning his methods for the sake of questioning, but I just want to understand his mind and ways,"* she assured Aunt Ruthie. To be honest it was an example of the critical thinking that was taught by Aunt Ruthie. It was not intentional, but Keila caught her mom off guard. Keila was one of the most caring and respectful young people that JT knew and he learned how to become better at loving others and respecting the deserved and undeserved too because of her. Yet, she didn't seem to display the skill that day very well.

Questioning what seemed to be concerning was one thing, but to question the Creators thinking and doing was something different and concerning in itself. Judging by the silence, Aunt Ruthie appeared stupefied and not able to reply momentarily. Keila began to appear uneasy herself. She knew that she had said something that didn't sit right with her mom, but she had a hard time computing why. JT started feeling it too. There was an imbalance between the three, which was usually not there. Unknowing was rare, but it happened when Knowers least expected it. Aunt Ruthie looked as if she could explode or implode at any minute. Keila grew more befuddled as the silence continued and burst into tears, unable to handle the feeling of frustration of unknowing any longer.

It wasn't blasphemy and the three knew that what had taken place was forgivable and could be thrown into the place where things are forgotten. A peace hovered over their heads that could not be explained. The force that Aunt Ruthie felt crouching over her earlier, protecting she and her daughter from what was trying to overtake them, stayed awhile longer until the danger was gone. The sharp pain felt near JT's heart was a sign of the similar circumstances that would show again and again on his journey. In he and Keila's youth was a significant innocence that was both strength and weakness. As less naivete took whole, their minds and hearts could be swayed to become good or bad. To keep the scales from tilting less favorably, Keila and JT would need each other all their lives or at least until the end of their individual journeys. Not only would they be grateful for the duality in nature, but so would their spouses and children. They were two parts of the same substance.

Although Keila wasn't part of the twelve at first, her time would come soon enough. Her studies at the university were almost complete. The seat at the table would be empty and the white cloth would have the initial K engraved perfectly in the middle. The privilege of guidance from the Looking Glass would not be afforded to Etta's niece. Yet, the gift of knowing was strong and would never leave her as long as she had breath in her body. The Spirit of Knowing hovered over the void and darkness around and within she and those that came before her, and she had heard stories of the first Knowers in her family that were more like she and Ruthie. Yet, the more unique Knowers came later through another blood line. JT and Etta were part of that clan. Together, both blood lines would benefit the world. In collaboration they made the world community a better place to do more than exist. The thriving upon the earth encouraged Knowers and Unknowers to remain hopeful in their journey in the known world and in the one to come. The mind filled with other-worldliness was less alert to the present journey and learned even less from the past. Knowers understand the importance of balancing whole knowledge. Unknowers relied on the Knowers' gift.

Chapter Nine

The call to go would come to her and she would go. The questions that always played over and over in her mind would be answered once she had taken her place with the others. The most difficult education to obtain would happen in the fellowship of the apostles. To secure it, she would have to walk through many fires. Her former self would be purged and made purer than she thought possible.

The path of JT and Keila was different from most Knowers, including Aunt Ruthie. However, it was the same one that Etta had taken, and it was the one that she would gladly do over if given the chance. Before JT and Keila took their individual journeys, years before they entered preschool, Etta knew it would come to past.

Their appetite and aptitude for, and attitude towards learning was the same with some minor variances. Keila learned through auditory, visual, hands-on, and through the classroom instructor and peer interaction best. Whereas JT didn't like school systems because of educational systemic problems that were not unique to only a few school districts and state educational programmes and preferred long hours of isolation and reflection.

No one was surprised to learn that Keila was recruited by some of the most prestigious educational programmes in the nation due to a perfect GPA, high scores on aptitude exams and IQ tests as shown in her school records, pre-school through secondary grades. When the small percentage of others in her small town were finishing two-year community college programmes, she completed a Bachelor of Science Degree. What was even more impressive, she was offered a fellowship to complete a Doctoral programme in Artificial Intelligence and Psychology. The total of time taken to earn both degrees, five years.

The expectations others had for JT and the aspirations he had for himself were a match. Equally, he would surprise them and himself with the achievements that he could have if only he applied himself to rigor and critical thinking. Serious analysis of any matter, text, or life itself was never a problem for him. It was the application within the confines of the system in which he learned, he found most disabling. In his eyes, he saw himself as a lifelong learner, the world his classroom and experience were his teacher.

The boardinghouse provided a learning environment that was comparable to any university in the world. His fellow eleven companions would agree. There was something new and advanced to learn each day.

Although Keila and JT's lyceums were stark in comparison and contrast, their goals were strikingly the same in every detail and required teaching, training, and the natural acquiring of education that was unique to Keila and JT Each were individual learners. Both were happy to go the way that knowing took them, but missed seeing each other develop along the way. Yet they knew that if they kept to the way as seen in the Looking Glass, they would be fine and together again soon enough.

No messages via pigeons, letters, postcards, telegrams, morse code, emails, nor texts were necessary. It was as if Keila and JT possessed twin powers, a form of telepathy of some sort.

The one knew the other and sensed the moments to pray for good health and for prosperity in all kinds of ways and in other appropriate matters. When the time was right or as it should be, they showed up for each other. Only the dark moments, those times when it was hard to see beyond the mental ambiguity and emotional disturbances did they seem so far apart.

The distance in miles was difficult enough, but the difference in approach to becoming the Knowers that they were expected to be in later years, was never quite understood by either one of them. Effected by the conjecture, the presumption to be or not to be, was certainly an equal challenge to both. Each struggled to see and feel the others direction at times and the challenge manifested itself physically and emotionally. Grandma Etta foresaw their experience in the Looking Glass with the wrestling of unseen and seen forces and hoped that with help from her faithful sister-in-law Ruthie, the two young Knowers, JT and Keila would be able to handle the trials and tribulations that would try their souls and will to be the best version of their Knower selves that was possible.

Both were strong and survivors, but knew that they had to reach a level beyond survival, one of thriving to avoid a complete madness takeover and the chronic fatigue that plagued more than a few Knowers. It was years down the road that each passed their own version of the test of wills. Neither would completely go mad, but would have temporary episodes of mental disability and neither became bedridden or wheelchair bound like some friends and family who were not so fortunate. That fact was not taken for granted. None were gladder than they were for each other's success against the emotional, mental, and physical disabling pandemic that had affected many Knowers for decades. Both acknowledged to each other in later conversations that the Knower way was not easy as was foretold in the Looking Glass. As with truth and the prophesies that were not found to be false, the words of the Looking Glass came to past. Both would sustain their sanity, health and wellness limitations until death would they part from a life of mortality to one of immortality.

Aging as equally well as Aunt Ruthie had in her late 90s, Keila afterward gracefully passed from the life of a flesh wrapped earth dweller were wars between flesh and flesh and those between light and darkness raged for as long as could be remembered, to be welcomed on to the beautiful landscape of eternity, to bask in the knowing of the great unknown. Her death from natural causes had been a gift from the Ancient One.

Found later in her abode was a journal left in her handwriting and it had been found sandwiched between her two favorite books, The Holy Bible and A Tale of Two Cities. It was important that her family knew what was in her heart and mind. The leather-bound pages were a memoir so to speak. It also served as a last will and testament. The things that she valued would be left to those that valued her in every sense of what it meant to do so. The first line read, *"outliving JT was the hardest thing that I ever had to do."* Apparently and maybe obviously this was written a little after JT had passed onto the other side. Saying those words out loud and writing them for public viewing had helped her stand firm in the little sanity that had not crumbled underneath the mental ground that held her emotional balance. Her greatest battle against the foe of sanity was a good fight and with faith in the Ancient One, she had won in the end. Together, she and JT had fought bravely and their final moments together were experienced victoriously, and the skill needed to win was not lost on the one left behind to face what life had to offer without the other.

Their connection had been severed at his last breath and the firing of the remaining neurotransmitters. Her favorite cousin and the one that knew her best had seemed to abandon her. She could not imagine going the way ahead seemingly alone and she wondered if the journey without JT would be worth the troubles that lie in the present and without invitation to the future too.

When the negativity of her reality hurt most, remembrance of JT's smile and easy approach to the way things were and the daily surrendering to it all made living the last leg of her trek through the jungle of life bearable, one similar to the Vietnam jungle that her dad Charlie had endured through emotional and mental toughness and faith in the unseen One. Holding on to the memories of her dad who had passed on to the other side a day after his wife Ruthie and five years before JT's demise, would protect her from the self-harm that came to mind often. All three voices and their spirits would be with her to the very end, her cheerleaders while she waited her turn to pass on to the forever world where they waited together patiently to greet her.

"You know who you are, walk in your faith baby girl," mama Ruthie and daddy Charlie would both tell her. *"Push through all the stuff. Pull yourself up out and above the quicksand,"* JT would say if he were around. She would reply, "*Amen*," and everything would feel that it was going to be ok, even if her knowing abilities conflicted with what she felt.

There were moments when she did not feel that she knew herself or anything very well. At times, she longed for blissful ignorance. The quicksand of madness was welcomed too as just a vacation from the burden of sanity. Brief moments of madness in place of clarity visited in spurts. To her big brothers, one spurt was too many. More than one was eventful and concerning on a whole new level. They joked that neither of them hardly knew her at all or at least which version of herself they would encounter when knocking and waiting to be turned away or invited into the home of the honourable Doctor, their baby sister. Keila and her brothers had wanted to forget the dark moments when their dad Charlie was away in a distant land fighting in the unpopular war. The unsparing battles fought on the homeland by their mother Ruthie meant that their parents faced struggles on two fronts. The loving couple were one and although they fought two separate wars they faced them together in mind and heart. As long as neither of the four children inherited the madness Ruthie and Charlie could be mostly assured of peace of mind knowing that they were spared its effects. None of them had shown signs while Ruthie and Charlie were alive. No signs meant a certain degree of blissful ignorance for the two loving parents. Ruthie had always been suspicious that it might remain hidden, but only until Keila experienced inopportune spurts of madness. Ruthie was right. The Ancient One had spared the mother and father in passing away before the spurts began. At the same time, the Omniscient One had prepared her brothers and Keila's longtime beau for the coming of madness spurts. She would need them more than she nor they would ever have known and there was one day when she seemed most lost to them that they all would have to prove their agape love for her. The speech that poured from her tongue and lips slurred as they dribbled and spilled in midair.

"Are you my God-sent cousin, mama, and daddy," was the words heard behind the French doors. Keila shook her head as she stood to the right side of the peep hole, listening for the right reply. The madness had come to claim her. Without JT and her parents, she could not function with the same

smoothness and clarity as before they were lost to her, the world, and called to eternity and the Infinite One.

JT had not known how to grieve for Etta's passing to eternity until closer to middle age. Keila helped him process the many years of sadness held within his mind and heart. It had threatened to tower above and engulf him in Tsunami fashion. JT returned the favor to her when they both mourned the deaths of her mother and father.

One secret that Keila took to her grave was the desire to pass to eternity before JT It was one of her few selfish desires and JT would have understood because they both knew the darkness that came with mourning for those loved deeply in life and lost to death. The loss to the void between the known world and the other world felt as if it was the ultimate final defeat to those that had loved and lost an important life and death tug of war. The Ancient One did not grant Keila's heart desire to pass JT in the race to the other side.

It had been a week since the celebration of life on temporal earth. JT's pictures were the few items that remained to remind the family that he once existed among mortals as one of them, imperfect, included. As per a written request, his ashes were scattered within the space that separated Grandpop's and Grandma Etta's grave. Although the breath and soul were long gone, Keila sensed a presence and maybe more than one, but she wasn't sure and one or all had lingered for a while longer days after.

No one knew that within her was a breaking point because she seemed to be so strong and unbreakable. There was a thin line between the emotional breakdown and sanity and the space was narrowing within her. As the spreading of ashes were mixed with the dust and soil, she almost gave in to the madness whispering to her. At the last possible moment her guardians, JT, Ruthie, Charlie, and Etta shouted at her from beyond the unknown and over the whispers of madness, "*STAND FIRM IN YOUR FAITH.*" The dilapidated Looking Glass was not in front of her revealing messages from the past and guiding her present towards a new day. Only JT was privileged to encounter the legendary power of the family heirloom and engage in its knowledge, understanding and wisdom. Keila envied him.

Through all of the occasional moments of the eventful celebration she appeared reserved, stoic, and strong. It was all for the others that she seemed all right. One of the few that sat with JT before the Looking Glass flickered for him, she remained until his girls arrived at the little Jim Walter Home to celebrate him and to listen to the last words of a personal knowing. As my sister and I took our place next to him, Keila, on cue left quietly to be with her thoughts and to allow her tears to flow freely in her own silence. She had told her big brothers and me and my big sister that she would be ok.

All of us knew that the honest verbalization of not being OK was better, but gave her some distance anyway and allowed her to explore her truth, to own it in her time. The space from everyone and everything would help and that's what we all wanted for her. The isolation would be temporary, and it would be a time of recharging her energy and a time of coming to terms with reality and the spirit of Knowing. No people in white coats would be called or sent to take her away. Beginning to slowly recover from the storm that had flooded her with fluid doubt and surrounded her with the angry winds that blew her off the grounded emotional stilts 'of life, her faith in the Ancient One weakened and fragile, the foundation on which all her Knowing was built, was beginning to slowly settle, and become steady again. Any misstep on the part of the family to mean well in their way of comforting her could cause a different outcome, a departing from the strength of Knowing to a dangerous and chaotic unknowing.

Keila's caring older brothers quietly stepped away beyond her space. Heads down, each brother backed down from intervening and interfering in her Knowing process. Like soldiers in the unknown war, head forward, all performed a crisp military about face, taking in with every breath what their sister seemed to be going through, hoping for an opportunity to slowly guide her to the safe zone, a place of peace, lined with fond memories of their mom, dad, and JT Neither wanted to be missing in life when she needed them the most. They knew how devastating that would be for Keila. Their dad had been missing temporarily in their lives when they were younger and then permanently gone forever and they had firmly decided in their minds to not allow history to repeat itself. Each in his own way would stand on the frontlines with their younger sister Keila as she fought her battles.

Uncle Charlie had not been there physically for Aunt Ruthie when she was fighting her battles against the enemy madness on the home front, but had prayed for her as he prayed to survive his own battles and return home with the scars to prove it. Guilt-ridden, he had spent many years trying to make up for time loss and for not being there when she needed her husband most. With Keila, he felt like he was being given a chance to prove his worth as a dad during her occasional emotional bouts too and in his remaining hours he wept that dying would rob him of many more chances to be there when it counted most.

Aunt Ruthie had never held the missing in action against

the love of her life, the daddy of her children. His baby girl, Keila had not held it against him either. Her love for him unconditional. The past had passed, and the present was all that would matter. The future was lurking around the corner, soon it would arrive with its surprises and inevitability. As her mom's big brother and her uncle, her cousin JT's dad was fond of reminding the family when he was alive, *"time waits on no one."* Keila knew that he was right in life and then in death. The wise words he spoke lived on behind him and was in a sense him in immortality. His unknowing was a gift in a way. It was painless and full of bliss. It was something that Knowers respected and appreciated on a very deep level within their minds and hearts.

If possible, a quick subsiding of the pain that came with knowing what she sometimes wanted to unknow as truth about time in the past, present, and future was desired. Often praying the poetic Psalm twenty-three had always helped in a time like the one she was experiencing. It seemed the best and right time in that moment of need to pray it again and more intensely than the last time her praying hands were put in motion. The pressure placed against the palm of the right hand against her left hand caused the flesh to darken as the blood rushed to circulate closer to the fingertips. She did this in silence and in reverence to the Ancient One. It was something she had learned from JT and it felt good as a spiritual practice.

In the last hours together, she and JT had prayed together and sang, *"it is well with my soul."* Keila had learned the tune and words from her mama Ruthie long ago and it was one that Etta sang to JT on his second day in the world. If the day would ever come, she would teach them to her children too, and she hoped highly that they would teach it too her grandchildren someday. She and her longtime beau had talked about and were still considering the process of adoption.

As a little girl, playing with her baby dolls she imagined having a family of her own someday. She knew what she wanted in a husband and baby daddy. Never abandoning her to loneliness and dark moments and thoughts he would be what she needed him to be always. At the end of their days together he would stay behind while she crossed over into the other world where she with Etta, her favorite uncle, Ruthie, Charlie, and JT would await his arrival.

The future was becoming harder and harder to catch up to and the past was falling further and further behind. The present had in one hand a baton from the past and in the other a baton to hand to the future. Keila and her brothers were Aunt Ruthie and Uncle Charlie's legacy that would be left to the temporal world for a few seasons. Each would play their part in the global drama.

One of the boys would work with their hands like his father. The other two sons would work in the field of technology. All three would achieve their own brand of success. Their younger sister had accepted her seat at the table of the twelve and saw her family only twice a year, Thanksgiving and Christmas. The oldest of Charlie and Ruthie's children had difficulty knowing what was happening to his little sister that was so much like their mom, Ruthie. Both mom and daughter always appeared normal, less superhuman when the unknowing usually happened, whenever anyone of them stepped out of the light so to speak and into a place of darkness. Keila seemed to be the one that was affected the most.

Many years before losing JT to the other side of life, the forever place, the family had worried about losing Keila to the present life where madness was in abundance. Adventurous, the lifelines in her hands stretched farther than Aunt Ruthie's, but there were things in life feared more than death, the deep unknown, which could swallow whole selves, its victim lost to a bottomless pit of void and senselessness. Aunt Ruthie secretly feared that Keila's intenseness, highly strung personality would correlate to her eventual undoing in the end. Similar traits of a worrying knower could cause her to slip over the edge and never return to the reality of the temporal world.

Aunt Ruthie was snatched back from its edges at the end of the Vietnam War. Almost slipping in and away when her hero reached out towards where she was falling. With outstretched hands, an Angel, Charlie appeared across the abyss, seemingly far from the edges. Deep of heart calling to deep of heart, he brought salvation to her, a better option than surrendering to the evil one and damnation. The world had been and would continue to be better off with Aunt Ruthie and Keila remaining in it during the time allotted.

Both had traveled extensively and seamlessly across social classes. However, traveling and consorting with unknowers and deepening a relationship with new Knowers had lost its appeal for Aunt Ruthie in her more mature years. The two Knowers that were most important to her were Keila and JT Each in their own way were destined to do more than anyone could have known was possible for two young people. JT's work was mostly done in New York City, and it was the one place that made Keila and Aunt Ruthie uneasy.

Receiving their blessing would have made the transition from the old life to the new one, his seat with the twelve and into the new and unknown experiences of what was known as the Big Apple less difficult. His departure from high school and the small town lifers had not been smooth either. Those first weeks in the boarding house were the hardest because he second guessed the decision and choice that was his to make as a new adult and it was one of the few disagreements that existed between him and his favorite aunt and cousin.

Aunt Ruthie and Keila weren't excited about his decision to move away and his choice of city over small town and neighbourhood location. To put down some temporary roots in which they knew due to restlessness uprooting would happen again later made little sense to them. However, it happened as Etta had prophesied. A wind had carried her baby boy from small town to big city and then to the place that never sleeps. Accepting this as truth didn't put Aunt Ruthie and Keila at ease and they differed in their reasons for feeling the way they did towards JT's decision and choice. What he did indirectly affected Aunt Ruthie because it directly influenced her baby girl in an unexpected way.

The seat left empty at the boarding house had chosen Keila long before JT had temporarily occupied it and she would only accept the honour in humility after his departure and extended absence. Her decision and choice to take her place among the group wasn't one to be taken lightly because the weight of entering into the discipleship could crush the unprepared in the modern world and beyond the present activities that were part of it.

Her parents would be left behind among the other small town lifers, but not forgotten. All the same, Ruthie and Charlie were unsure that she would not forget herself and become someone and maybe something else. Although she was not the same seemingly fragile little girl that was born so much tinier than her older brothers, nevertheless she was still their little girl.

The parents reminisced about that day and the conversations with the doctor afterwards. Both worried about the size of Keila's head in comparison with the rest of her body. It was disproportionate, but the doctor assured them that all was well and that the body has a way of naturally balancing itself.

Just as predicted, she grew into her head. Like most kids she was teased a lot about her differences from others. Although her big brothers made fun of her before it was no longer disproportionate to the rest of body, they never allowed other kids in the neighbourhood nor school to do the same. At home, they would use intentional puns like *"don't get any big ideas or don't get ahead of yourself,"* then they would all laugh. At first it would make her so mad, but after a while she became tougher, and she learned to come back with something funny and clever of her own. When JT came over they would turn their antics towards him. Keila would laugh and then help him with a few come backs. It took a while, but he learned how to play the game. Keila's older brothers grew jealous that the two were so much alike and they started calling them the twins because no one ever saw one without the other usually.

As they grew older everyone in the family realised that both were outgrowing their little part of the planet. Neither would be satisfied with the smaller happenings in life. Each knew without much proof that there was something as big as the ocean, space, and time. There were more in the unknown than the experiences that could be offered in the watering hole of a home that limited their exploration of imagination. No pun intended, they were both heady and high minded and knew that what seemed unknown never remained that way for very long. A lover of science more than JT and anyone that he knew, Keila was exactly what the twelve needed and wanted. JT had played his role in bringing her to them. Like the giant in the bean stalk story, what he valued had been taken from him. The giant size heart that beat within him was broken again, but it wouldn't be the last.

Like Etta, his favorite cousin had meant so much more than anyone who did not have much of an imagination could imagine. No pea brain, head in the clouds, she was the best friend that he needed and would always need. After his mom's passing they grew closer and shared their small and big dreams and ideas with one another as if no one else mattered in the world. It was true that their bond was strong and Keila assured him that it was stronger than the one she shared with her brothers and the twelve. He knew that it was true too and knowing it made him uneasy. The madness was trying to affect his heart and mind. The twelve were not stealing her from him. Jealousy was a tool of darkness and he had to overcome it, especially if he were going to succeed in the city that never sleeps.

Like JT, his favorite cousin would abandon their small town life for bigger dreams and thinking. Ruthie and Charlie were sad to see her go but knew that the day would come when Keila would. Her brothers joked one last time, *"don't get any big ideas or don't get ahead of yourself,"* and then they all laughed. No quick mouthy come back, just a teary look towards the grown muscular men, who pretended that something had crawled onto their eyelashes and it was hard to wipe them away. Clearing his throat, the older brother stepped forward as representative of the others and hand presented a small box to their little sister while the other two brothers loaded her car with bigger boxes.

As a philosopher, she adjusted easily to new ideas that

informed innovation. Her tech-savvy brothers were excited to share with her their knowledge of the new gizmos that made receiving information and communicating across long distances easier and faster. The smaller box contained a beeper and the bigger ones packaged new technology.

Computers were becoming popular among the masses just before the turn of the next century and something new was invented that made sharing data and knowledge within anyone's professional and personal life easier. If these new technological advances and modern forms of communication would have been available to Uncle Charlie and Aunt Ruthie during their time apart, maybe Aunt Ruthie wouldn't have been affected by the Knower's touch of madness or maybe she would have recovered much sooner while Uncle Charlie was away.

The letters between them often crisscrossed one another in midair on Air force planes and mid-ocean on the Navy's ships moving latitudinally and longitudinally. By the time the letters arrived at each sender's address the conversation was old and outdated, the questions were reduced to rhetorical meaninglessness and the answers were no longer sought. Without the connection usually felt through in-person contact or over-the phone voice recognition, relationships seemed less than what they formerly were.

To each other, Aunt Ruthie and Uncle Charlie were missing in action. Their hearts had been broken then and fast forward to their present day, they felt a great sadness that Keila and JT had broken contact with them for extended periods, their work and calling took them to distant places. It was hard on all four because of the darkness sensed during those times. However, the three Knowers felt the longing for the missing in their lives most intensely before it happened and once those deeply saddening experiences had past, reflection commenced, but then it felt as if they were late in response to the needs of their family members. An unknower, Grandpop had felt this intense knowing briefly as he held Etta in their last moments together. To be one in matrimony was truly felt and given new meaning.

Like many unknowers, Uncle Charlie had always been at a disadvantage to the Knower ability to know before physically seeing a thing happen and being touched in mind and heart through an unworldly experience. In the world he was and being of the world was always difficult to resist and it distracted him from knowing the otherworldly events happening all around him. It was a blessing and gift for him to be attracted to one who was the opposite of him in the ways it mattered.

Aunt Ruthie like most Knowers was better at pushing away the things that they saw first before it was too late and the parts of herself that she treasured were guarded. Also, like many Knowers she suffered because without warning most times she could not save some of her most treasured things from the ugliness that came with the touch and eventually the engulfing of darkness. She and Uncle Charlie treasured their children most and longed to protect them and repel anything that could possibly and potentially harm any of them.

Their matrimony seemed preordained and their oneness seemed easier than it actually was. They played it cool, but the facts were clear for both loving adults. Knowers being married to Unknowers had its share of problems. The biggest one was the difficult absence and what seemed like the temporary breaking of ties. The bond was still intact, but it seemed to be severed during extended times a part.

Uncle Charlie experienced it in Army Basic Training the

first night as he laid on his bunk alone. Away from Aunt Ruthie's touch and no longer able to hear her breath in the night. He did not understand until after Aunt Ruthie explained in her letter reply what she knew to be truth about herself and the deep love for the one she was supposed to share every moment with. It was at that time that the touch of madness began to affect her. As long as she was connected to the one that she had said the words to, *"for sickness and health, through death do us part,"* the madness was kept at bay.

Their letters of reply to each other were consistently sent a few days apart from each sender's current residence, Uncle Charlie's training facility and the house that he bought for his family to reside in he hoped for generations. Once Uncle Charlie was shipped off to the place where the battles of the unpopular war were being fought, Uncle Charlie's and Aunt Ruthie's letters were consistently less in arrival and the lag in reply time increased. It was as if dark forces were at work and play. They worked in Aunt Ruthie's mind and played with her emotions. Mental fragility was the Knower's enemy.

Keila experienced a touch of madness away from Aunt Ruthie and JT and so did they when away from her and each other. The three gentle giants in their time knew that being away from each other and the others that they loved deeply for too long was their kryptonite. Separation in families of Knowers and unknowers was something that was weaponised by the dark forces for as long as could be remembered through verbal and written accounts among family historians and professional storytellers.

Anthropologists concurred with those findings as accurate scientific data evidenced in results found on papyrus scrolls and symbols on pottery and cave dwellings hidden away from the unknowing inhabitants of every continent. Later, companies were formed to tackle the subject of DNA evidence and results. It was discovered that every person that had ever lived and live in the world presently, Knower and unknower were and are related distantly. All are connected through their life-giving blood.

It is weird to think that two people gave birth to humanity's billions of persons on earth. Not everyone believes this to be true and subscribes to alternative faith. In a survey given to Knowers and unknowers, in an even split, 50% of participants believed in the creation theory and 50% were certain that aliens from six worlds across millions of light years across space were responsible for the different ethnic groups on the six continents of the earth.

As one of the twelve, Keila's purpose was to lead the research into the phenomenon and arguments on either side of the subject. JT promised to help her gather data through surveys and interviews with willing participants among some of the hundreds of underground citizens in New York City. The birth of the internet made it possible for JT to send the information via something call electronic mail, but he preferred to scan survey documents to a fax machine instead of trusting the U.S. Postal Service snail mail.

Keila lit up with excitement when she received the first email from *jtimes1@hotmail.com*. It was a personal note. *"Hey Keila, what's up? I'll try to write as much as I can before my dial up connection drops. It can be slow getting it going again. How's the family doing back home and at the boarding house? Everything is cool here literally and figuratively in the city that never sleeps. The leaves are turning orange, yellow, and red and the high winds are scattering them from one end of the city to the next. It's all good, but I'm going to the thrift store today to get a reasonably priced coat, jacket, sweaters, scarves, and skull cap. You know me. I get cold easily. It might be that I need to eat some good cooking and put some meat on these bones. Tell Aunt Ruthie when I visit her and Uncle Charlie that I can't wait to taste her soul food! Got to go, but I will write again soon. In the meantime, drop me a note and oh yea, I'll have to tell you about this new thing I'm checking out called a chatroom. Love you much cuz."*

Keila had mixed emotions about the electronic mail received from JT because it was short, and it left her wanting to know more about what was going on with him and she was thinking about visiting which was unusual for her because she was never one that traveled very many places, especially one that made her feel so uneasy. She was still thinking of how happy it was to hear from him but that she was a little sad too because she missed seeing his facial expressions as he verbally expressed himself with purposeful long pauses in between as he thought through carefully what to say and how to phrase what would be said next. All this came to mind as she began to type her reply.

"Nothing much JT just thinking of how much I miss you man. Still learning to use this alien technology (she knew he would know what she meant and laugh). Do you remember the 10th grade typing class on the typewriter in Mrs Bailey's class? thirty words a minute was my top score, and I almost barely passed the class, but I was happy that she let me do a ton of extra credit to bring it up to an A. Don't be jealous, but I think I was her favorite student (she knew it wasn't true, but she wanted to mess with JT who really was the typing teacher's favorite student and Keila always teased him that maybe their

relationship may have been inappropriate, and his facial skin would turn a purple red every time she made the comment)."

They both had excelled in the computer class offered the next year, but the prerequisites were typing one and typing two. Keila was better at Algebra and wanted to learn more about computer programmeming. JT was interested in computer science and the inner workings and parts of the machine too. Before Keila could finish her email reply to her favorite cousin, the internet connection in the public library disconnected prematurely.

While the librarian tried without much success to reconnect her to the poor internet connection, Keila browsed a fashion magazine. She drifted into a daydream about New York and the adventures that JT could be enjoying or not and the way the natives of the big city probably dressed. She imagined there were fancy sweaters, dresses, skirts, pants suits, high heels, and sexy underwear designed for the modern woman of the mid to late 1990s. The thought of all the variety of clothing alone overwhelmed her visual sensibility. She was a combination of non girly and an intellectual type. All of what New York had to offer to the tourist and others escaping their dull humdrum of life did not appeal to her.

The fun of discovering new knowledge and widening the boundaries of her worldview mattered more than the worldly trappings that most women of her age group found hard to resist and then escape. Most women of her peer group would say Keila's wardrobe screamed 1980s for most of the next decade. She was starting to think that maybe a change was due. JT had always been the adventurous one that welcomed change more easily. She couldn't wait to tell him in her email, but it would have to wait. The dial up wasn't working, and the librarian told her to try again in a few hours or the next day.

A few years later, she was among the small number of computer users living in a medium size urban community that graduated from dial-up to broadband use. Efficiency was always important to her because having better meant that she could do better. Technology at the end of the 20th century had improved exponentially and had made her life much better than she could have imagined ten years prior.

In the 21st century, she wondered how she lived without VCRs, IPODS, cell phones, GPS, WIFI, and the 42-inch flat screen coloured television that sat on her dresser in the room at the boarding house. Growing up in the 1970s and 80s in her small town, those electronic gadgets were imagined and dreamt of by futurists and inventors, but most naysayers would never concede in their thinking nor out loud that the advent of those things were possible. The practical use of any inventions was motivation enough, but the wealth and riches discovered in consuming those inventions encouraged brilliant minds to look further into the desires of the world's inhabitants. Companies found ways to combine media, maps, video, etc. onto one gadget to keep the consumer's attention focused on what was possible to have. The less naysaying the more they said yes to buying what they desired or thought they desired, and the more money salespersons made.

Most Knowers were old school and only bought what they needed most of the time. For example, JT still used phones connected to landlines ten years after cell phones became popular and affordable for regular customers. There must have been something about the number ten. All of his shoes, clothes, televisions, radios, etc. were ten years old.

Keila preferred receiving the news of the world through the

television because she got it faster from the television anchorman and reporter than from the newspaper staff. She didn't trust the news that came from the internet unless it was verified by her favorite trustworthy live news personality. She and JT would discuss and scrutinise different news topics over the phone and through emails too.

Each evening she received her updates on current worldly affairs before meditating and then laying down for a good night's rest. The next morning, she arose to stretching exercises, more meditation, prayer. Afterwards, she anticipated what news would be brought to her at the start of the new day. Yesterday, she received good news that JT was returning to their small hometown to visit.

He didn't know that she knew why he chose to go back and that this would be the final time. New York and all those he had helped were left behind him. Ahead of him was the uncertainty of life on earth and the time remaining. He had slipped quietly away in the night, under the cover of darkness while most of the city residents were settling into their usual nightly rituals alone, or with friends and family. Sensing that it would be good to take a train to New Jersey and then pay for the bus fare from there to his small town. After arriving and receiving his ticket for the 8am bus departure, he decided that he would sleep for a few hours with one eye opened and then reach out to Keila via pay phone when he awoke to the annoying sound of his battery-operated alarm clock. It had been set to sound the morning news show. There was some hysterical talk of attack on American soil in New York City.

Keila pressed the television remote button to turn the volume up as she stared wide eyed at the news anchor who had revealed what was known at that moment of the plane that had been strategically flown off its flight path into the twin towers. There in front of her was an unbelievable event that she had not prepared her heart and mind for. Throughout elementary and secondary school years and as part of training at her important job, she had been prepared for tornadoes and other eventful and uneventful disasters, but what was called terrorism had baffled her. As more news reports poured in on each channel of the television, it seemed that she was not alone in disbelief of the strange occurrence.

While she struggled to mentally digest it all her Samsung B690 flip phone rang. She assigned the Space Odyssey ringtone to JT because he seemed to be always spacing out lately. She pressed a button to speak and paused and then she heard his voice, *"Hello, Keila, you there?"* Finally, she managed to say, *"hey."* JT heard the muffled sound of measured crying and imagined what she must have been feeling after seeing the news of the destruction and people's charred bodies and others leaping to their deaths. Uncomfortable with sad, fearful scenarios and light conversation, he tried to sound cheerful and even made a bad dad joke.

Without much small talk about the day and weather she got straight to the point. *"JT, I know."* Caught off guard, he stammered…*wwhat you talking about?* JT could tell in her tone that she was frustrated with what he had thought was best at the time.

Keila was disappointed too. The Ancient One had not answered her prayer with a definite and definitive yes that she would journey to the other side of life before JT Instead, the opposite was coming true.

For good reason, dad had tried to hide from Keila his war with bad health, fought on three fronts for as long as he could.

The battles with madness, the virus demon, and the cancer beast were intense until the last struggle to breathe, the dreadful sign of life ending. Everything to him was always a matter of fact, he convinced himself that it was the way of the world. Conflict, wars, rumors of wars, and death were inevitable.

Grandma Etta had lost her war with bad health, the final battle with the demon virus. Grandpop's cells had waged a civil war, the bad ones winning every battle against the good ones, leading to his demise. Aunt Ruthie, Keila, and dad throughout their lives experienced a common enemy pushing against the gates of their mental fragility, trying to conquer them with weapons of madness and destruction.

The good news for Keila was that Aunt Ruthie and Uncle Charlie had died of natural causes according to a final report from the coroner. Also, JT promised Keila that he would not hide his prognosis because not sharing the diagnosis had hurt their relationship. Keila reminded dad of their pact to stay on the earth together for as long as humanly possible, no giving up too early, no going away too soon.

JT solemnly replied, "*I know, I'll try.*" Everything else he heard over the pay phone at the bus depot was *"blah, blah, sniffle, blah, blah."* He felt more sorrow for her and those that would be left behind than he would ever feel for himself. Their remaining journey would be longer and filled with more of the same worldly stuff; greed, suffering, conflict, foolishness, knowing, but never fully understanding, and unknowing leading to undoing of good.

He smiled as he thought of Etta, his Pops, Aunt Ruthie and Uncle Charlie. It wouldn't be too much longer. He would say hi to them for Keila, her brothers, and his brothers and sisters too. A peace came over him that he had never experienced until then in his lifetime. At that moment nothing else mattered. No words and language could be spoken to describe that moment. A familiar voice was heard over Keila's in the phone receiver and it was loud enough to drown out the voices in the large station. As if needed and on cue, the voice was replayed over the air through the intercom system, bouncing from wall to wall; *"youthful strength will take you far and wisdom will be your guide through life's rollercoaster journey."*

Before long another voice was heard over the intercom reminding him that his journey from Jersey was about to begin. The bus attendant seemed to be an Angel in disguise, helping the passengers heading west and south depart towards their desired destinations. Keila was disappointed that JT couldn't remain on the phone because it was attached to the depot wall and couldn't be detached and taken with him on the bus. As a minimalist, JT had opted to only use landlines to call her and although she didn't understand his philosophy regarding the chosen lifestyle, she chose to respect his choice.

Chapter Ten

It had been a long time since dad had been back in the old Jim Walter Home. It was empty, abandoned, beaten, and whipped by aging and inclement weather. On the outside and inside it could use some work and it all needed to be done while he had strength and before Keila arrived. The cosmetic stuff dad could do by himself, but he would need his big brothers and cousins to help with the bigger repairs and renovation, including the leveling of the foundation and floors. It was Grandpop who had taught him, his brothers and cousins about construction and carpentry and had bragged about the good bones of the Jim Walter Home. The smile on Grandpop's face when he made the proud statement was unforgettable because he hardly ever smiled, especially not as wide. A smirk appeared on dad's face thinking about it. It was one of the ways he and Grandpop were different. One was a joker and didn't seem to take anything very seriously while the other seemed to be quickly concerned about everything and was always preaching against what he called joke-lying and foolishness.

    Dad's brothers, sisters, and cousins were better at joking than him, but he improved over the years, and everyone was surprised because they always thought that he would be less of a comedian as he aged because he always had this way about him that reminded them of Grandpop. Yet, dad had a way of reminding them that he was also Etta's son too. She was always reminding Grandpop that one writer in the bible said that laughter was good medicine and then she would tickle his side and they both would laugh and even do a little wrestling.

It was what dad was missing in middle age; someone to tickle him and to wrestle with. He had intentionally dated women that were the opposite of Etta because he feared that they would leave him. Always on alert, he probably missed out on the woman of his dreams, his soul mate.

Being back where life started for him brought back so much to his mind that his heart nearly burst being so full of emotion. All the years of worrying about others had weakened the important organ and slowed its beats considerably. The cardiologist last measured its function and warned dad that if it fell lower than forty that could be a sign that something was wrong with his heart. When dad replied, *"Yes, I was born with a broken one,"* the heart specialist gave him a half smile as a reward for his ability to joke during such a serious moment. If he had known his patient's family history, he would have known that dad was dead serious.

Being back in the place where he lost his first love to death stirred more than the nostalgia lurking in every corner. So much so that it nearly knocked him off balance. The couch that could be considered antique and past its prime was nearby and still able to do the job it was made for and that was a good thing because with the big renovations done the crew had gone home to their families.

No one was there to care for the one family member that needed caring for the most. The one that had cared for so many others had neglected his own health. The battles with illness had got the best of him and retreating back to friendly territory was one of the wisest decisions he had ever made in his entire life.

The dizziness subsided as he lay still as a corpse. Looking

down he saw one of the other signs the heart specialist had warned him of. The swollen puffy ankles didn't look like his own. Closing his eyes he hoped that when opening them again that the nightmare that he called most of his life would be over.

In half nightmare and half dream, he saw himself being almost pulled into two parts before being let go and then he went across a bridge where he found his forever home. There was singing and the smell of honey dew all around him. These were the two things that made him forget all that he had lost in the life behind him.

Then Etta appeared to give him the bad news. It was not his time. He wasn't dead yet. He was only near it. Etta assured him in her motherly way that going back would be bittersweet. There was a little more work for him to do and a few goodbyes too. She pointed down and he saw that his feet were no longer swollen and next to him was his favorite cousin calling to him.

Waking up he felt as if he had been sleeping for eight hours or more. He felt both glad to be alive and disappointed to return even if only to finish his time and work on earth. When looking strangely at his surroundings and then at Keila he felt shame. He wept allowed and Keila tried to comfort him. *"I've been a fool. I stopped caring about what matters and made everything about me,"* and then the dam broke, the tears overflowed and his body quaked again uncontrollably. Suddenly something happened that had not happened in a very long time. A familiar voice was heard in the room and a writing on the wall had begun as well. As the voice spoke the writing began and continued.

Both had witnessed the flickering across from the couch together, above the black and white 12 inch television set that was perched on a 3-foot-tall oak bookshelf that Grandpop made himself. The electronic parts within no longer worked, but the old television was kept around for nostalgic reasons. Its rabbit ears were made from a metal close hanger long ago, now rusted.

Much like dad's birth, youth, and strength, when first created, it was a marvel to the world, it held up for as long as it could and was useful for as long as possible. Like the old television, he began to feel his uselessness increasing, his inward parts no longer what they used to be. Most of the cells in his body were in chaos, out of control, lumping together as an ugly mass of tissue and there was nothing that could be done about the progression of his sickness, and he thought it was best to hide it from the family for as long as possible, except for Keila, who always knew.

The mind melding with Keila left dad and her at a disadvantage. Secrets were between, but never kept from each other. To her amazement, like Etta in her remaining time, it seemed that all that was left of him were the few healthy brain cells and some movement of limbs. Etta's walker and wheelchair in the shed outback were always on standby as a main mode of transportation for the Jim Walter's sick and shut-in.

Bringing them to him, Keila asked dad if he would be OK for a couple of hours while she ran errands. Without looking in her direction, he smiled while nodding his head up and down, acknowledging that he had heard her question and yes, he would be fine until she returned. Lifting an object in the air, he waved it as she turned towards the exit of the little room. *"I have everything I need,"* he whispered while placing the journal into his lap. The words that his daughters would read later when he was gone would be printed in his favorite-coloured ink, green apple was what he called the colour.

Within the soft brown leather-bound pages would be a story of a birth long before dad's own existence into reality and it was one that he thought his babies needed to be privy to. Although dad saw us as his innocent little girls, we were adults and could handle its contents. Neither of us were Knowers and both of us were more like our mother, and dad was happy to realise that neither would be touched by the madness that skipped Grandma Etta, but her baby boy was not so lucky.

Only those touched by madness understood its effects within the mind and soul. The day before his youngest son left home, before his death, grandpop dreamt about the madness and those that it touched, and they would meet the little boy he loved so much. The emigrants going and the immigrants coming, lived in New York City and they needed dad because he understood what was happening in their minds and soul, the restlessness.

Our Cuban mother was one of the lost ones and needed to be found by him. Most men who saw her were immediately spellbound by her external beauty and would do anything to impress her. It was not so with dad. When they first met in the mid-1990s, the only thing dad owned was stuffed in a military duffle bag, and there wasn't love nor lust at first sight. Something deeper caught his eye. It was the longing in hers that drew him in, and the mesmerizing would hook him and hold him steady. However, she wanted and needed more than what any mortal man could give her. What she thirsted and hungered for was not of the physical world and could not be gifted by any person who wanted to be bound with her as a friend and life partner.

Although it was clear to her that he wasn't her type, he had a good heart and for a while that would be enough. Mom and dad's first date was over dinner at the new boarding house, *Rest Your Feet*, in China Town. Thirty days later they agreed to marry so that she could remain in the country and so that dad would no longer be alone. Drawn to dad's kindness, it was enough for many years until it wasn't.

Mum understood the English language better than she spoke it and dad helped her speak and write it better as well as check the boxes on the requirements of becoming a citizen. As a proud independent person, it was hard for her to accept the help my dad offered and questioned at what price this help would come. It was difficult to trust that he wanted nothing more than friendship, a weapon against the loneliness and madness he battled daily.

Dad's acceptance of mom's nonbinary identity in terms of gender and sexuality won her over, but her thirst and hunger for more than what he could offer lost her to him, my big sister, and me. The gods of her world required the sacrifice of those she valued more than anything else. Their marriage and our family were torn asunder, never to reunite. Dad was never the same and refused to remarry because, in his words, *"she was my God-sent wife."*

The men in my father's family love their women deeply and when the person they love are taken from them it is one of the most painful moments and experiences of their entire lives. Dad had hoped for the forever kind of love like the one between Uncle Charlie and Aunt Ruthie and Grandpop with Grandma Etta. That love never came to claim him, but he clung to the hope that it would someday before the future becomes present and time ceased to exist in the temporal.

Once life had gone into the past, there was no reverse button and no proverbial time machine that would help return a person to a lost moment. Those that valued dad's existence always reminded him of the importance of present living. Looking back and dwelling on the things that were no longer worthy of his focus was forbidden. Ahead, there was a lot more for him to do and all would be contingent upon what lay in the present. As a young man, dad was so indifferent to much of the politics in life and memories of his upbringing encouraged him to remain so. The family, community and culture that cultivated mom's view of life and the world taught her to fight for much more than anyone wanted to give her.

What had dad given her? *"Two of the most precious babies known in creation,"* she always remarked. So, why did she leave preciousness and kindness behind? *"Love is why,"* she said to her seven and nine-year-old girls. It was self-love that she referred to. She loved herself more than she loved anyone else, including a good man who had given her good girls.

Within five years she had built a new life with someone else who could give her the American dream that her family back in her native country had always told her was hers if she wanted it and shouldn't expect anything less than she deserved. A letter came in the mail one day for dad and us to read together. It began with an apology for not writing sooner, but she had been busy preparing for the day when she could offer her girls something they were worthy of. The day had come, and she was ready for me and my big sister to move in with her and her new husband. The letter further illustrated how different mum and dad were and that mum truly was from Venus and dad from Mars.

Losing her was devastating to dad. Gaining what she believed she deserved meant everything to mom. The three of us never understood why we weren't enough, everything. When the letter came it was a heavy reminder to our mind and hearts that she was the winner, and the rest of us losers. We could forgive her for leaving and giving her physical self to another husband and to the god of material things, but we had hope that she would allow us the peace of forgetting, allow us to leave that dark memory locked in the deposit box, under guard. The three of us as if on cue huddled together in our little two-bedroom apartment and cried. The last few lines of the letter made us dreadfully aware that our hope and dream of her returning would not come true because our dream conflicted with her dream.

The commonality that existed between mum and dad was that both wanted full custody, but would let their girls decide. For one of the few times in his life dad felt like a winner because we chose him. We were proud of our mother for not being a sore loser. Graciously, she accepted our choice, her loss.

Like Uncle Charlie those many years ago in Vietnam, she was recruited and left to go far away. For a long time, she had gone missing while fighting her battles, but unlike him, she would never return to the one that believed her to be his *"God-sent wife."* Her girls would never see a better her and would never hear her use the word love when remarking about her feelings for them in a sentence ever again. Dad was dead to her, but she would never say that to him, nor would she allow us to hear her admit it. Conditioned to feel fear, anger, and passion; remorse, sadness, and compassion was what she could not feel. Dad had found her in a dark headspace, and she seemed grateful and happy for a few years for the distraction from her goals, the reasons she had come to America. Once her thoughts of getting what she believed she deserved were jogged enough to surface, those old tendencies to do whatever she felt she had to do to enter the rat race and remain a contender for the prize, she took her chances even if it meant sacrificing the most precious in her life. Losing her girls was less important than losing herself, the fighter, the winner. Our dad was not her equal in the way she needed him to be, and she believed she deserved better. In her mind, he never fought for her and even if he had he would have lost.

If she had known him better, she would have known that she was wrong about him. A fierce fighter for the things and ones he loved he was the better man for her. He didn't know that she didn't know what he was willing to do for her. If he had truly known her, the part of him that knew how to make dreams come true would have switched on. He would have done whatever he needed to do to show her how much he loved her. The minimalist and indifferent side of him would have been discarded. The introverted part of him would have been murdered and the extrovert part of him would have been given full reign of his entire self. There would have been a willingness to become what he was not, but with free will, he could become. Within him, there was something that called out for more too. Perhaps it was that thing that drew him to her. Like him, she had felt the deep within herself calling to the deep within him too. They were a match in that way only. In all other ways they were complete opposites. Heartbroken, dad unwillingly went his way as she went on to what she saw as her discovered long ago higher calling.

My sister and I discovered too that we were more like mum than our dad. The deep calling within guided us to what we thought was our destiny as well. Throughout high school, we worked hard and maintained perfect grade point averages. My big sister received a letter officially accepting her into Harvard with a full scholarship. Although dad wasn't a big fan of school systems, he expressed how proud he was of her success in navigating secondary schooling and now she had earned a post-secondary opportunity to become and do what she felt she deserved. It was that part of our mother that she possessed, and dad appreciated. However, unlike our mother, she wasn't willing to sell her soul to the devil or sacrifice her babies to an unknown god. Like her, two years later I shipped off to an Ivy League School, Yale University, supported by a full scholarship and my dad's blessings.

Like Grandpop and Etta had lived through their children, dad and mum lived through us. Our successes were their successes. Both attended our high school and college graduations. Eventually, they learned to be cordial towards one another again. Mom's new husband respected dad. Neither felt uncomfortable nor threatened by the other. It was OK to be OK with one losing and the other winning. They both loved her in their own way and there was no sense in denying that. Manning up to the reality that lay between them was important to both. Any jealousy and animosity between them had to cease because it was the mature thing to do. Burying the hatchet was good for everyone for many reasons. One that was most important would be revealed at an opportune time. In the meantime, they knew that the present time was as good as any time.

The two men had once been best friends. Mom's new husband was the reason dad had gone to New York City in the first place. Their friendship had started when dad began visiting him in prison. Eventually, he was freed after being exonerated. The state prison down south compensated the prisoner and restored his unblemished reputation as a good citizen. Innocent of state charges, but guilty as charge in stealing his best friend's wife. To his credit, he had not intentionally meant to hurt dad, but as much as mum and dad had little in common, the ex-prisoner and mum were a better match in more ways than one.

The small-town lifer had escaped to the big city, but didn't fit in there anymore than he did in his hometown. Dad's giant heart could be seen a mile away by the nearest New Yorker, who were known for their big aspirations. Maximalism was the word that described the culture. Anything that was done was done with the motive of getting more of what's deserved or getting ahead. Dad was the opposite in thinking.

Like the ammunition that Uncle Charlie remembered whizzing around him in what seemed from every direction on the bloodied battlefield within what were once rice fields, the blurred faces of New Yorkers and tourists raced past him every day, nonstop. Each of them seemed the same kind of person and were after the same hidden buried treasure. X marked the spot on the maps that they carried within their hearts and minds. All willing to do whatever they needed to do to find it and possess it. Nothing was off the table. The sacrifices made were never too large.

The giant within him was being pushed around by the little thieves who were willing to take until they were caught and scurried off down one beanstalk and up another one to do the same to some other unsuspecting victim. The worrier in dad worried more about those that took from him than for his welfare. He didn't stop worrying even after the mark of the cancer beast showed its signs. His slowed pace became slower. The dry cough increased and when my sister and I would ask him to see a doctor, he would *"joke that he would stop smoking."*

We knew that dad had never smoked in his life and that

joke was his way to disarm tense situations, but we were suspicious that something was going on that dad didn't want us to know. We tried not to worry, but it was hard not to think the worse. Although my sister and I didn't have much in common with dad, like mom, we were drawn to his kindness like a moth drawn to a flame.

He was a good father and provided what material things he could with his meager earnings. Most of what he had went to my sister and me when we were younger and while we were in college. He valued our happiness more than his own. He believed that he should give us an inheritance before he passed on to the other life and believed that he would give us plenty because as far as he knew, he had plenty of time and inheritance left to give. I'm not sure if he would have done anything any differently if he knew that he had been short on time and inheritance.

I think my sister and I would have lived our lives differently and realised that his minimalism was better than our maximalism if we had known the value of the time and inheritance given by our father. Although he was always sharing little bits of kindness with us all the time, we grew even more suspicious about what was happening with him because the kindness increased it seemed in every way. Every good thing we did was singled out.

The acknowledgements felt good to receive but, in a way, they seemed unearned and undeserved. Sometimes my sister and I would discuss how it made us feel to receive such precious nuggets from dad. The emotions were mixed with anger and bliss, but always a see sawing from one to the other. It was as if something was awakening in both of us. It was hard to explain, but there seemed a knowing beginning to show itself and it confused and frightened us. The hidden things about dad were starting to become unveiled.

Dad had always seemed a little mysterious to us. We always thought that he was just an odd duck. More often than with my sister and me, dad's aloofness bothered mum and other people who loved competition and social indulgencies and were energised when around a crowd with similar tendencies. Yet, he was cool in some ways that our friends' dads weren't, and we appreciated that. His genetics contributed to that part of our creative genius. It is that part of us that draws others to us, some for good reasons and other people for not so good reasons.

Dad had talked about the many personality types that we would probably meet when we left high school and went into the world to continue our education. Some would remind us of the people we had known our whole lives while others would add to our collective experiences as well as add variety and spice to our lives. Each in their own way would come and go at the right time.

All would leave their mark and take what they needed from us, something of value to them. Strangely, it all happened the way he said it would. His experiences in his youth had been similar to ours and now at the end of his life, he would have more in common with his precious Mama Etta than with his baby girls as he lay ready to receive from others, but more so to give to them.

There were very few to count that came and left dad with gifts and receiving from him in return. He had remarked once or twice that each time it happened it felt like Christmas. The things he would say always left me feeling that there was something hidden between the lines of his sentences.

Words spoken from his mouth were usually meaningful

and small talk was never his thing. Listening closely benefitted the listener and dad appreciated the attention to details too. Mum had always said that *"he just like hearing himself talk and that every word was coming out of the side of his neck."* I tried looking up the *side of the neck* reference, but was unsuccessful in discovering its definition, but did uncover its Ebonics origin.

Recognizing her foul mood, I didn't bother asking her what she meant. Plus, the other words that followed from her full Afro-Latina lips were of much more colourful language than usual and required a more accurate translation of the combination of Spanish, Spanglish, and very little English. Under breath, I managed to mumble in between mom's ranting and raving that a lot of soap was needed to clean her filthy mouth.

Grandma Etta wouldn't have approved of dad's choice in mate, but I have a sneaking suspicion that Grandpop's grandmother would have loved my mother. Grandpop had married Etta, the opposite of the woman he nearly hated, but after he found religion, he believed that she at least deserved agape.

Dad met her briefly when he was very young, not long after Etta passed. Without saying goodbye, she moved back to the reservation in Oklahoma. No one knew before Grandpop received a letter. In it were a few lines referring to her call back. The Great Spirit had her number all her life and decided to give her a ring. Though Grandpop never really understood her and had every reason to disapprove of her personality he was never heard voicing it. The family knew what kind of person she appeared to be, but never knew her heart. Still, no one would have blamed Grandpop if he had chosen to not want a relationship with her. Her aggressiveness and pride were attractive to some men and a turnoff to others. The most unattractive part of her was the nastiness that showed when she was in her worst mood.

Dad often imagined what her people were like and if they felt like strangers in a familiar land whenever they left the reservation. The pioneers had become the citizens of colonies and then decided to make it a permanent home and call it a nation, a united one. They became united against a common enemy, the original citizens who were corralled and told to live as a nation within a nation. Dad wondered if there were a prophet among them; one that would lead them out of exile and into a promised land of their choosing. He mused if they had it in them to rise up and fight the last great war; one that was justified unlike the unpopular war that Uncle Charlie was forced to fight in. Maybe they would not have shed any blood. A peaceful leader could rise up instead and become Mayor of Oklahoma through one of its powerful political parties and then set his sight on capturing the White House without violence.

If dad could talk to his great grandmother there would be so many questions to ask. The questions would be similar to the ones he had asked my mother about her people. He had wanted to understand her and where she came from. The conversations between him and she were always brief and left him hungry for more information. There seemed to be intention in those brief interactions. Dad's intentions were birth from the pure of heart. My mom's intentions were sinister in nature. There were things about her that it was better for him not to know. Leaving him in the dark was on purpose and in a way, she was being good to him by protecting him from the ugliness and darkness that she escaped from and before being deported back there she would rather die free of its reality. She had planned her escape long before she met my dad, but had hoped to meet someone like him that could help her realise the American dream.

A stowaway on a cruise ship for a day, mum kissed the Florida shores literally and then wept, made the sign of the cross and then found a pay phone next to a convenience store and called the number of a contact. In Spanish, the man spoke rapidly, giving her specific instructions of what to do and where to go next. No need to write it down, she had always been able to memorise large amounts of information quickly. It was one of her superpowers. It was one of the only gifts that my sister and I had gotten from her, and we used that brain power for good.

We understood Spanish, but never spoke it often and our mum said that we should because it would be the dominant language in the world someday. By the time my sister and I were in high school, we realised that we both possessed the superpower of linguists. Understanding languages came very easy and speaking each after only a few lessons didn't seem a big deal to us. In high school and college, we decided to focus on French and Mandarin.

Neither of us could have ever imagined in a million years the value of being linguists. It would get us a seat at the table with some very important people. Having an Ivy League education was great, but the linguist skills were a bonus to our repertoire. There was more to us than meets the eye and it felt good to possess that kind of power. The part of us that made us our father's children were the Angels on the shoulder that spoke to our conscience when we became too prideful and fixated on the perks that came with superpowers. We learned to speak less about ourselves, especially our achievements, and more about the things that mattered most to others.

Dad knew what we had accomplished before it happened. Like Grandpop, he was gifted with dreams about those that he loved and felt close too. He saw our wealth and the joy that came with having our superpowers. He also saw that we would be strong and not easily overcome by the temptations that came with having so many blessings. What had made our lives already rich was his unconditional love and consistent encouragement. Our lives had already been planned before we were born. Everything we were supposed to experience happened with a purpose in mind. Dad always said, *"girls, keep your eyes wide open and to never shut them even in fear of seeing too much."*

Grandpop had given him the same advice and that it was something Etta had told him to pass along to him when he was ready to hear it. It was written in a card for high school graduates that Grandpop had asked the Walmart clerk to assist him with. He was never good at that kind of stuff, but was good at asking for help when he needed it. My Aunt, dad's oldest sister helped Grandpop write in it the words left to dad before his final breath. Dad's big sisters waited till after Grandpop's home-going celebration to give their graduate gifts along with Grandpop's to him. Tears of sorrow and joy flowed it seemed incessantly and then the streaming dried and then without warning he fell on his knees and then into a child pose. Both sisters knelt on either side of him and all three remained quiet for a while. It was a perplexing moment for them because there was a sadness because their dad was gone, but joy that he was finally united with love ones gone before him and then there was joy that his prayers were answered to see all of his children graduate high school and to live his dreams through them.

Grandpop had wanted so much for his children and had

received so little for himself it seemed. However, those that knew him best would say that he had lived well and had been given more than he had imagined could be possible given his background and upbringing. Because of him generations would be blessed with more than they deserved. Through his and Etta's gene pool a population of humans would do better than his generation. They would know more and go further in mind, soul, and spirit. Their lives would be better. The world would be better too. Etta had always talked of the coming of a better generation. Grandpop had always believed that if Etta spoke to listen and if she said that it would happen it was already done. He was glad that she had said everything that he needed to hear because he sometimes waivered in his faith. Not just faith in the Ancient One, but faith in humanity too. There had been so many egotistical acts witnessed in his lifetime and less selfless ones. The meanness in the world had increased and seemed to be the dark cloud that never went away and would choke life out of the sun if it could.

His mom, my Great Grandma, had told him many times to dream of better even when it seemed that he was wasting his time and prayers. Before meeting Etta, no one else had any bigger faith. When she was a young girl, faith and dreams kept her hope of better days alive and kick'n. Grandpop had known poverty, but not the kind that his mum had become very familiar with. The meals were hit and miss, but some days they had to be stolen and it wasn't something she was proud of, but it was just the way it was. Some of the women in her community would trade their little girls and boys for the price of two to three good meals a week. It was the end of the first great war and the good times never came even after many years of praying. The suffering was difficult for her to speak of and she said that her mama sacrificed more so that she would not have to.

Dad's love and appreciation for his grandmother knew no bounds and she could do no wrong in his eyes. Through hard work and hustle she did what needed to be done so that Grandpop, her oldest son, would have better than she had at his age. Her little girls would never fear of being given to older men because culturally and for reasons that had to do with survival it was the right thing to do. They would be given the chance to marry for love. Their love stories would end for better and some for worst, but at least the opportunity for love existed. Whatever the circumstances they found themselves, their mama was cheering for them equally.

Her grandchildren were her pride and joy too and she wanted them to dream bigger than their parents dared. Nothing would be too good or big for them to have if they wanted anything. When reminiscing about her sometimes dad would drift off in thought. He missed her. At the end of the summer, just before he went into middle school his grandma said goodbye to him and his siblings. The reservation in Oklahoma was calling to her because it was time for her to go home. Dad had cried and begged her to stay, but she told him not to cry and that he was welcome to visit. He never saw her again after that day and often wished that she would have taken him with her. When he was in ninth grade, he wrote a poem that he shared with his literature teacher, entitled I Lead the Cheer.

Stand with me as I lead the cheer with enthusiastic fervor
Make the noise to be heard to inspire
Sing with me as I lead the cheer that shakes the earth's core
Breath and rhythm felt in nature's choir

Give me a S for the sons who brave the world when hopelessness stands before The goal and the prize is far off in the distance

Run towards what waits in the great unknown, but is yours for the taking and more

The valued bringing joy, laughter, and a dance

Give me a D for the daughters who are strong facing the anguish of adversity

The fight is never easy, but the battle won

Never deflected in intention nor waiver pressing onward to what is guaranteed

Praise be given to what could not be done

It was as much of a tribute to his grandmother as it was to all her generation and yet dad didn't think it was enough. Generations that came after them would have to show that the sacrifices made would not be in vain. Dad was never sure if his generation could ever measure up and could carry the torch as a symbol that the game of life would continue. The division between the Knowers and Unknowers gaped more and there seemed to be no way of reversing it within his generation. The poem written in appreciation to his grandmother could easily be read to his generation to encourage togetherness. Together they could do anything that they put their minds to. They could go farther and become what others only hoped could be. Letting go of the grudges would be a start, but so much more could be accomplished than what's on the surface of relationships or lack of.

Dad had always questioned in his heart what he was willing to fight for and to run towards in the long distance. The past, present, and future had always pulled at his coat tail beckoning him to see beyond the time and space that could never be known. The answer to what mattered and what was worth fighting for and running towards no matter how far it was and where it led in a lifetime could be discovered if Knowers and Unknowers searched together.

Dad had always said that going deeper is the key to unlocking the unknowing door. Our subconscious knows something that we haven't discovered. Somewhere below our conscious marks the spot where the treasure lies waiting for us. For Knowers, it was what kept the madness away and could separate high thinking from low thinking. Unknowers were capable of inventing and creating once the light bulb switch was found and turned on by their counterparts, the Knowers. Life's mysteries could be uncovered and made available to anyone who was searching for the clues to knowing beyond their imagination. The missing reality of what links Knower to Unknower could be right in front of them.

Unknowers were God-sent to Knowers and vice versa. Unknowers who married other Unknowers were at a disadvantage in the same way that Knowers who married Knowers were too. The Ancient One had not made only one kind of human for a reason. Variety had always been the spice of life. Humankind was made to meld minds and walk in harmony as what was and will always be known as humanity. Segregation and division, the enemies of the natural process of humane togetherness and human kindness must always be fought back behind enemy lines or humanity will face down the barrel of extinction and its territory forfeited.

The madness was known to start civil and global wars and is the culprit that could be what causes the breakdown of civilization. To keep it at bay agape must be practiced without ceasing and weaponised. Novice historians can see the signs of potential conflict mapped throughout the story of the world.

It starts in families and then spreads like a pandemic throughout communities and spills over into foreign borders. After the damage is done everyone goes back to doing what makes them happy and forgets the lessons learned or not learned. Then before anyone knows that it is happening again the Cains attack the Abels, the Hatfields the McCoys, the Bloods the Crips, and one Colour of Skin against another…

Dad had always told me that the first humankind were different. Together, they moved in rhythm and cadence like Uncle Charlie had learned to do with Aunt Ruthie before he marched with other unlikely and likely human soldiers. Dad had also told me that with each other, mingling together, Knowers and Unknowers were likeable and their best selves. Without each other, Knowers and Unknowers were just nice people that one may not necessarily trust at first sight.

Honestly, being nice was not something dad was genuinely good at. On the other hand, generosity and compassion were more of his strong suit. Dad had learned how to be a good man through those that came before him, the gentle giants on whose shoulders he and his siblings and cousins stood.

The heads of household in the family did more than pay their fair share of taxes to the internal revenue service. All of them had big hearts and only wanted the chance to do good in the lives of their families while they could. Neither ever really understood the other at times, but they knew that they were kin to each other. Great Granddaddy, Grandpop, and dad were different in some ways, but very much the same in other ways. Their approach to life was consistent in every instance, even in self care.

The holistic approach to caring varied between them, but the mind, body, and soul were important to the representatives of three generations. Good physical and mental health served their purposes. To dad's two girls these concepts were worth pursuing for obvious reasons, who agreed that sometimes going off the traditional beaten medical path was necessary.

Our dad was never known for his conservative approach to health and wellness and neither of us were surprised when we saw in his chicken scratch the instructions of final days of care, *"girls, no, this isn't a will and testament, but it is my will to be in comfort and have a quality of life at its approaching end."* We followed what he willed in every detail. The tea and the pills were administered simultaneously. We wanted to make sure dad spent his remaining days in comfort. My sister and I were second guessing him and ourselves about what to do and if we should follow his instructions, from the moment it was decided what the comfort measures would be. Each day he seemed to stir less and less. For a while, we both feared that the mixture of Native American and western medicine would have less than the desired effects. However, the carefully prepared cocktail of peyote and medical marijuana was effectively pleasant. The hours of slumber seemed to be extending beyond the norm and expected until the unanticipated happened. The cough, followed by indistinguishable phonetic conversing, prematurely interrupted my sister's selfies and uploads.

He spoke some sentences that seemed nonsensical at first and then they were not once we made sense of them. Dad drifted off again as my sister checked her social media account and the sweet lady from the nursing agency sat near the bed. Before the home health hospice nurse left for the day, I took advantage of the moments of silence when dad slept soundly without interruption. Walking the lawn, so many things came to mind. I imagined dad, my aunts, uncles, and cousins playing together, laughing at the silliest things, but most of the time he would be alone gazing up at the stars and staring into space, hearing a calling, waiting for what was next.

He was in many ways like his dad. Before his time in some ways, Grandpop was smart, creative, hard-working, and never wasted anything in his life. He must have been one, a minimalist before it was a cool coined phrase by hipsters of my generation, many of them had never been fragile, poor, broke, nor had stood anywhere near the poverty line. I realised as I took in my surroundings with small inhalation of breaths, my dad had experienced all three.

Simple construction and landscape ideas, the property was without a fence and everything within its borders was basic in every detail. Everything around me, including the sparse shrubbery, seemed underwhelming and insignificant, frozen in time, like someone or something in cryostasis, awakened later for a purpose to be revealed at some point. After a while, I felt as if I was being called to certain areas of the outdoors to take inventory of the exterior spaces that my dad and his family had been privy to. It was as if I could hear the childhood of many being replayed in the drama of small-town life. *"Tag you're it,"* a youth's voice suspended in mid-air, near a grassy area that looked familiar. Walking over to where I thought I heard the sound of laughter and there I remained a little bit.

Standing under the huge oak tree, the yard seemed so small in measurement and the 900 square foot construction once inhabited by dad's family sat in front of the hundred-year-old tree a little to the right and it seemed no bigger in width and height fifty-four years later, one month to the day of dad's birthday and Grandma Etta's death day. There it was in my reality, a Tiny Home out of necessity, unlike the prefabs purchased by later generations downsizing for convenience and for some, easier mobility. Nothing had changed, the paint was still the same colour, a little worse for wear, flaking and faded. It was exactly the way Dad had described it in what seemed countless stories of his home, in his contemporary time. It was reminiscent of what life must have been, stuck in a time that had passed and the structure could use the help of celebrity home renovators.

The old Jim Walter home was not constructed with a beautifully designed exterior door with a knocker and doorbell at the disposal of the occasional visitor. Knocking loudly at the entrance's keyhole stood my mother with her new husband and in bad taste I joked, *"is that you mother with your God-sent husband?"* The knocks at the door were very few although I had hoped there would be an influx of those that celebrated my dad's life with my sister and me in the little space that had been his childhood home.

They trickled in one at a time between days and weeks, none stayed very long, nor did they return after the one visit. Each saw him through their own eyes and memories. In another life, he may have been a negative or positive influencer of millions. Most of his reality, and during the life that I knew of, he walked in the shadows. As a nobody, he was invisible to the self-righteous, whose light shined what seemed as brightly as the sun, in comparison to the candle he held.

Who he was, wasn't hard to grasp in understanding by those who knew him best and saw that during his life on earth he was shrouded in transparency. One could blame genetics. Misunderstood for most of his life by many, dad was mysterious, strong, and feared for being either and not predictable. To some, he appeared overconfident and loved himself too much. Unknowers had always expressed their disdain for dad and Knowers thought that maybe he was too vain for their taste. At the end, two handfuls of people visited his bedside to pray with him and to genuinely say that they loved him unconditionally despite his many flaws.

During his short life, dad was never nominated as Mr Popular in the family nor among his peers. An eccentric and one who could be accused of the use of vocabulary painstakingly, the list of things that made him well liked, were very few indeed. His politeness had always made me both smile and frown because I was never sure if he was being respectful or manipulative.

When he spoke and I would remember it to be one of the last sentences to me, I chose not to debate within myself what seemed so unimportant in the time we had left. I often struggled with knowing because of my struggle with being both Knower and Unknower. One tear lay at the corner of each eye as he stammered the words, *"b-aby, w-ould you be so k-ind to put my wal-ker close-r to me?"*

I was surprised to hear him speak and I repeated the request back to him while standing next to where he lay. The underused muscles in his arms had a difficult time aiding in efforts to leverage the rest of his body's weight, barely, the strength in them were enough to grab hold of the walker next to the bed. Slowly he rose, his legs buckled slightly, he paused for a moment before continuing.

I asked, *"how do you feel?"* It would be the last time that he would leave the room and walk the short narrow hallway. He joked that he had *"never felt better, and it was nice to be back down to my high school weight."* One could see that his figure wasn't boyish, but more resembling the persons seen in photos as prisoners housed in concentration camps.

As my big sister and I stood on one side and dad's two big sisters stood on the other side of his bed of affliction, dad seemed at peace, the wrinkles in his face and the crow's feet, usually as noticeable as his beautiful eye lashes seemed to fade. The incredible story of his life had been written down long ago. *"Almost ready to drift into deep sleep,"* he whispered as loudly as was possible for him to do.

Fifty-four years in the past, he had peeped into the room from the hallway where his mum sat waiting for assistance from his dad, to rise for the last time from what coupled as her bed of affliction and the launching pad from temporal time into eternity. Now coming full circle in time, on the same bed he lay. He, a worrier knower, had gone as far as allowed. The cancer and viral beast made sure of it.

If he had a do over in life, he wasn't sure if he would do things differently, surely not worry less. There was no shortage of people and things to worry about. While still mulling over purposeful intentions and tension in that critical juncture and the decisions made in moments of knowing, a flickering began in a familiar space of the abode.

The dilapidated mirror on the wall had been forgotten. It had seemed to lay dormant in activity until that moment. Mother and son, both gifted with knowing, their time had come again.

Young Etta stared at the wrinkled face of the man that looked vaguely familiar to her. JT stared back at the young woman that closely resembled someone seen only through flash backs. The Looking Glass captured their reflection from time and time again. Each life flashed before the other's face like the motel vacancy sign seen late in the night by weary travelers and passersby. Both, knowing full well that their lives were somehow intertwined and passing in the night simultaneously and welcomed each to rest.